Eben Edwards Beardsley

Life and Times of William Samuel Johnson, LL.D.

Eben Edwards Beardsley

Life and Times of William Samuel Johnson, LL.D.

ISBN/EAN: 9783337055486

Printed in Europe, USA, Canada, Australia, Japan

Cover: Foto ©Raphael Reischuk / pixelio.de

More available books at **www.hansebooks.com**

LIFE AND TIMES

OF

WILLIAM SAMUEL JOHNSON, LL. D.

Wm Saml Johnson

LIFE AND TIMES

WILLIAM SAMUEL JOHNSON, LL. D.,

FIRST SENATOR IN CONGRESS FROM CONNECTICUT, AND
PRESIDENT OF COLUMBIA COLLEGE,
NEW YORK.

BY

E. EDWARDS BEARDSLEY, D. D., LL. D.,

RECTOR OF ST. THOMAS'S CHURCH, NEW HAVEN.

NEW YORK:
PUBLISHED BY HURD AND HOUGHTON.
The Riverside Press, Cambridge.
1876.

LIBRARY
UNIVERSITY OF CALIFORNIA
DAVIS

RIVERSIDE, CAMBRIDGE:
STEREOTYPED AND PRINTED BY
H. O. HOUGHTON AND COMPANY.

PREFACE.

No one will think that I have stepped beyond my province to write this volume. The life of a Christian layman is not an unsuitable theme for the pen of a clergyman; and the delineation of individual character, when it is made subservient to the cause of morals and religion, is an employment, the importance of which cannot fail to be generally recognized. Undoubtedly it would be better for the youth of our land, if in the multiplicity of books more fondness were shown for those which inculcate the great lessons of practical duty, and less fondness for works that furnish ideals of goodness and excite the imagination without teaching the due restraint of the appetites and passions. Biography, rightly prepared, is a species of literature which will impart both pleasure and instruction.

It has been said by a great English author that " they only who live with a man can write his life with any genuine exactness and discrimination." If this were true, biographies for the most part would be valueless; for not many have been written with the advantages of personal knowledge. My own interest in the history and character of the subject of this volume is of comparatively recent date. It has grown mainly out of readings in the direction of the fortunes of the early Episcopal Church in this country, and especially in Connecticut; and it seems strange to me that a name so distinguished among the founders of our republic should have been left for more than half a century with no other record of its deservings than brief sketches in periodicals or meagre notices in biographical dictionaries.

Like his venerated father, Dr. Johnson was in the habit of preserving the original draughts of many of the letters and documents which he penned, and but for these no such picture of his life and times could have been given as that which is now offered to the public. His long residence abroad at a critical period of American affairs makes that part of his correspondence highly valuable; and if new light be not thereby thrown upon the events which led to the Revolution, they will yet be seen from the side of a judicious and careful observer, and present in a new aspect the blind and impolitic course pursued by the government of Great Britain towards the aggrieved Colonies.

I have not thought it necessary to introduce in full more than two of the letters which were printed in my " Life and Correspondence " of his father, but passages have been taken from them to connect the narrative and support the statement of facts. The book might have been increased in size by publishing more of his correspondence while he was in England acting as the agent of the Colony of Connecticut; but the observations and views addressed to Governor Trumbull appear to have been communicated with entire confidence and freedom to his father, and it would have been very much of a repetition to have printed the semi-official papers along with the family epistles.

His Diary, begun after his appointment as a colonial agent and continued until his return to America, has guided me to some important materials, and enabled me to go in and out with him as he visited the King's Bench, the Houses of Parliament, and the great and good men of the realm, whose acquaintance served to cheer him in his weary sojourn. Though showing to a limited extent the manners and customs of the period, it is almost too fragmentary to publish; besides, as the better portions of it are given and enlarged upon in his letters, the publication seems to be uncalled for, particularly in a work of this kind.

Dr. Johnson lived nearly fifty years after his return from England, and the largest share of the more dignified and interesting events of his public life falls within that epoch, and blends with the sources of our national history. No special information has come into my hands in regard to his connection with Columbia College. The archives of the institution are without printed or manuscript memorials of him, and I have been obliged to gather the facts I have used concerning his Presidency from the letters and papers of the Johnson family, which have been kindly left in my possession since the publication of my " History of the Episcopal Church in Connecticut."

The engraving was made expressly for this work from a portrait by Gilbert Stuart, now owned by Mr. Charles F. Johnson, of Owego, New York. My thanks are due to several gentlemen for supplying me with dates and letters which have enabled me to bring the volume to a more satisfactory conclusion.

NEW HAVEN, *November,* 1876.

CONTENTS.

CHAPTER I.

CHAPTER II.

CHAPTER III.

CHAPTER IV.

CHAPTER V.

CHAPTER VI.

CHAPTER VII.

CHAPTER VIII.

CHAPTER **XIV.**

A. D. 1800–1817.

CHAPTER XV.

A. D. 1817–1819.

LIFE AND TIMES

OF

WILLIAM SAMUEL JOHNSON.

CHAPTER I.

BIRTH AND BOYHOOD; PRELIMINARY EDUCATION AND ADMISSION
TO YALE COLLEGE; GRADUATES AND BECOMES A LAY READER;
LETTERS TO DR. BEARCROFT; RESIDENCE AT CAMBRIDGE AND
DEGREE OF MASTER OF ARTS FROM HARVARD COLLEGE; RE-
TURNS TO STRATFORD AND COMMENCES THE STUDY OF LAW;
LEGAL SYSTEM OF CONNECTICUT AND HIS APPEARANCE AT THE
BAR; MARRIAGE AND SEPARATION FROM HIS FATHER.

A. D. 1727–1755.

ON the 14th day of October, 1727, the Rev. Samuel Johnson, of Stratford, made an entry in his private
journal in these words: "This day, I am 31 years
old, and this sevennight (Oct. 7,) it hath pleased God
of His goodness to give me the great blessing of a
very likely son, for which, and in my wife's comfortable deliverance, I adore His goodness." What there
was discernible in an infant of seven days, to warrant
such a description, may not be readily apprehended,
but WILLIAM SAMUEL, for so the child was christened,
proved "a very likely son" indeed, and filled in fut-

1

ure years the vision of his father's highest hopes and anticipations.

His boyhood was wholly passed under the parental roof and watched over with the tenderest solicitude. From the dawn of intellect, he was under gentle promptings and a judicious guidance. His mother was a daughter of Col. Richard Floyd, of Brookhaven, Long Island, and the widow of Benjamin Nicoll, Esq., by whom she had two sons and a daughter. Her children by the second marriage are the subject of this volume, and WILLIAM, born March 9, 1731. No parent could be kinder to his own offspring, than was Johnson to his step-children. He superintended their preliminary education, and gave the sons a better preparation for collegiate studies than the schools of the time supplied. He was a skillful teacher, whose training for the employment was begun in Guilford, his native place, immediately after completing his academic course at Saybrook. During the turbulent and unhappy period of transferring the Institution from that place to New Haven and establishing it there under the title of Yale College, he held the office of first or chief Tutor, and only retired from the position upon being ordained to the work of the Congregational ministry in West Haven. The change in his religious views and his subsequent settlement in Stratford as a Missionary of the Church of England did not diminish his interest in educational matters, and it was natural, therefore, when a family of sons came to his care, that he should wish to instill into their minds the elementary principles of knowledge, and to advance them according to his own model of instruction. In order to make it more pleasant by giving them companions, he himself says, that "he took several gentlemen's sons of New York and Albany," and thus added to his pastoral labors what many of the clergy of that day were obliged to perform, the task of becoming classical teachers to fit youth in their parishes for admission to college.

When the celebrated Dr. Benjamin Franklin wrote him in 1751, and tried to persuade him to leave Connecticut and assume the headship of what is now the College of Pennsylvania, affirming "that talents for the education of youth are the gift of God, and that he on whom they are bestowed, whenever a way is opened for the use of them, is as strongly called, as if he heard a voice from heaven," Johnson in his reply said, "I have always endeavored to use what little ability I have in that way in the best manner I could, having never been without pupils of one sort or other half a year at a time, and seldom that for thirty-eight years."

No extraordinary incidents have been left on record concerning the lads of Johnson's household. Undoubtedly they played on Stratford Green, and had their sports like other boys, but of any precocity or special indication of unusual strength of intellect, we are not informed.

William Samuel Johnson was entered a member of the Freshman Class in Yale College, and graduated a Bachelor of Arts in 1744, just ten years after his half-brothers — William and Benjamin Nicoll — had been admitted to the same degree in the same Institution. He must have been well prepared for the course, since his father said of him, and of his other son, that it was a great damage to them that they entered so

young, and that when they were in college they "had
so little to do, their classmates being so far behind
them." It was a matter of regret with him that he
had not previously given them instruction in his favorite Hebrew, a study which it was not possible for
them to pursue in college with any advantage, for
want of a competent teacher. The father fixed his
hopes upon his first-born son becoming a clergyman,
and his early religious character gave promise that
he might be led ultimately to this decision. The
rigid law of the Institution during his connection
with it allowed no such indulgence as is now granted
to Episcopal students in public worship, but he was
permitted to go "home to church, once in three
weeks," if possible, or once a month at least, to be at
the Communion ; and from a regard to the wishes of
his father other little relaxations of the law appear to
have been granted him by the Faculty, as far as they
were able to do so "without hazarding the resentment
of the government that supported them."

He was scarcely seventeen years of age when he
graduated and received the distinction of being
elected a "scholar of the House," under the bounty of
Dean Berkeley. When he returned to the parental
roof, it was to pursue the studies of which he had
only laid the foundation in college, for in a letter to
a friend from whom he had expected a visit, written
early in the summer of 1746, he speaks of the want
of literary society. Two of his classmates resided in
the town, but one [1] of them had married a wife "from
such a family as forced him to avoid any very great

[1] **Agur** Tomlinson, who married the daughter of Rev. Hezekiah Gold,
Congregational minister at Stratford.

familiarities," and the other was of uncongenial tastes. " For this reason," he said, " I but seldom go abroad, and am obliged to content myself with the company of those who have been long dead ; to search the Latin and the Grecian stores, and wonder at the mighty minds of old."

He now added to his other studies that of Hebrew, and aided his father in his missionary labors by acting as a catechist and reader for the church people in Ripton, and received for his services an allowance from the Society for the Propagation of the Gospel in Foreign Parts. He penned a characteristic letter to Dr. Bearcroft, the Secretary of the Society, dated March 27, 1747, which is worth producing in this connection to show the nature of his youthful fidelity. " I beg leave to return the Honorable Society my most humble thanks for the kind notice they have been pleased to take of my services at Ripton, and shall endeavor to answer their intentions and expectations to the utmost of my abilities so long as I have the honor to continue in their service. I have now, at the earnest desire of the people of Ripton, read prayers and sermons in that parish a year and a half, where there are above 50 families of the Established Church [Church of England], and catechised their children, which are 150 fit to be catechised. They live so scattering, that I have been obliged to attend them at several places, and almost from house to house the last winter, it being impossible for the children to come together, by reason of their distance from one another and the badness of the weather ; though I hope in the summer season they may meet for that purpose in the church, which the people have with considerable expense and labor lately plastered, so that it is now comfortable and fit for the performance of service in."

About a year after this, he wrote again to Dr. Bearcroft, informing him that when he first obtained the Society's favor, he was undetermined what course of life to pursue, but, having entered upon the study of the law and decided to prosecute it at least for some time, he relinquished the allowance made him as a catechist, and gave notice that he could not serve the Society "longer than till next Michaelmas." The letter was closed with a significant paragraph: "It is not impossible, but I may hereafter alter my views and desire to enter the service of the Church, which, if I should, I shall be extremely obliged to the Society for any future notice they shall be pleased to take of me."

It was before he had come to this determination that he set out for Boston, and arrived there on the 30th of May, 1747, intending to spend a month or two at Cambridge, hear a few Lectures in Harvard College, and be present at the Commencement to receive the degree of Master of Arts. In those days wigs were fashionable, and worn by persons who had no necessity for them, simply because they were fashionable. They formed a part of the dress of gentlemen, especially on high occasions. Young Johnson wrote his father from Cambridge, in anticipation of his appearance at Commencement, that he had spoken for a wig, and could not procure one under £10; everything being "monstrously dear" in Boston. His Master's degree cost him more than he had anticipated, but the grant and the charge were united by the Corporation, and if he took the one, he was obliged to submit to the other.

The correspondence between the father and the son, at this time, is full of affection, and dwells upon his vocation and prospects in life. Before he returned to Stratford, he had made up his mind what he would do, and planned for the future with the wisdom and forecast of an older head. In entering upon the study of law, he had not the advantage of being directed in a systematic course, or of consulting many text-books and works on jurisprudence and political history. The legal system of Connecticut was then exceedingly crude, and the manner of proceeding in the trial of causes was less definite here than in the province of New York. He addressed a friend[1] in that government, and said he was convinced " that the practice of law must be infinitely easier in New York " than here, and added, " In our pleadings and arguments, our practicers are obliged to rely upon their own imagination and draw from their own stock, oftentimes a most miserable resource. There," he continued, " industry, application, and a good collection of books in general, does the business; here, a teeming fruitful imagination, will make the best figure."

He seems to have pursued his studies upon a large and liberal scale of his own devising, and to have prepared himself to enlighten, if he could not change, the irregular equity by which the courts were guided.

---

[1] William Smith, a graduate of Yale College, 1745, author of a history of New York, and a member of the Council of that Colony. Late in the Revolutionary War he joined the cause of the Crown, and finally settled in Canada, where he became a Chief Justice.

His first appearance at the bar of Connecticut forms
an important epoch in its legal history. Instead of
an occasional recurrence to a few of the older common law authorities, which had been respected
rather than understood, he cited them frequently and
put them in the stronger light of a more complete
elucidation. While yet a beginner in his profession,
and much in want of books, which were scarce in the
country and costly, he saw advertised for sale in New
York, Viner's "Abridgment,"[1] and mentioning his
desire to possess it, his father gave him forty pounds
for the purchase. He mounted his horse and rode to
New York, and brought back the volumes as far as
then published, and at once commenced a thorough
study of their contents. "And those books," he said
to his son later in life, "were the foundation of my
learning in the law." In the New York "Evening
Post" of November 16, 1819, a writer, familiar with
the incidents and labors of his life, says of him at the
period above mentioned : —

"Dalton's Sheriff and Justice of Peace, and one or
two of the older books of Precedents, formed the
whole library of the bar and the bench. General literature and taste were, if possible, at a still lower
ebb among the profession. Mr. Johnson, gifted with
every external grace of the orator, a voice of the
finest and richest tones, a copious and flowing elocution, and a mind stored with elegant literature, appeared at the bar with a fascination of language and

---

[1] Viner's *Abridgment* — original edition, nineteen volumes folio — is
still in the library of his grandson, at Stratford, Mr. William Samuel
Johnson, from whom the above anecdote was obtained. His grandfather's
autograph appears on a fly-leaf of each volume, with the year of the
purchase.

manner which those who heard him had never even conceived it possible to unite with the technical address of an advocate.

"At the same time, he rendered a still more important service to his countrymen, by introducing to their knowledge the liberal decisions of Lord Mansfield, the doctrines of the civilians, and afterwards (as more general questions arose) the authorities and reasonings of Grotius, Puffendorf, and the other great teachers of natural and public law."

Thus he took at once the highest rank in his profession, and became the renowned and high-minded advocate who was always crowded with cases, and had his clients in New York as well as in every part of Connecticut. The distant seat of the court in another county was reached at that period by the slow stage-coach, or by the traveller's solitary ride in a chaise, or on horseback, and his physical constitution was often in this way put to the severest test. "I have always," wrote his father from New York, on one occasion when he knew his son was absent from home attending court, "a sort of terror at the sound of Litchfield ever since the sickness you got there. I shall long to hear you are well returned."

His settlement in the domestic state was a step surveyed from the Christian side, and early taken. He had scarcely passed a month beyond his twenty-second birthday when he married Ann, daughter of William Beach, of Stratford, a wealthy gentleman, and a brother of the Rev. John Beach, of Newtown, so celebrated for wielding a controversial pen, and for his unflinching adherence to the Church of England during the stormy times of the Revolution. A friend,[1]

[1] William Smith.

to whom he had not previously communicated his matrimonial intention, though his correspondence with him had been quite extended and intimate, was writing him shortly after the event of his marriage, and having first taken him to task for his secrecy, said : " I heartily congratulate you upon your marriage with a lady whose fortune, though it has made a considerable accession to yours, did not so much recommend her to your choice as those virtues and graces which made you esteem her the ornament of her sex."

The militia system of the Colony was the right arm of public defense in those days, and the services of the citizen soldiery were held in high and honorable repute. Influential and prominent men were chosen to the offices of different degrees, and the people respected them and encouraged the feeling that was alive to ward off danger or to resist the invasion of a foreign foe. Mr. Johnson, apparently as much from a love of it as from necessity, shared in the military spirit of the time, and was commissioned by the General Assembly, at its May session in 1754, as a Lieutenant in the first company of his native place ; and afterwards, to apply with a verbal change the lines from Cowper's immortal ballad, —

> " A train-band Captain eke was he,
> In famous Stratford town."

His respect for the wisdom and learning of his father was intense, and occasionally they were found mutually advising each other in the work which pertained to their separate occupations. In 1754, a movement was made in New York to erect King's (now Columbia) College, and the projectors fixed

upon the Rev. Dr. Johnson, of Stratford, for the first
President, and sought his aid and counsel in shaping
the scheme and putting it into effectual operation.
It was designed to conduct the Institution on the
broad principles of Christian liberality; but the con-
tentions which arose before the charter was perfected,
and the violent opposition of a few leading members
of the Presbyterian persuasion, were discouraging features in the affair, and exposed it to some peril. As
the son would not himself be concerned in any disputes with respect to the College, so he desired his
father to "stand perfectly neuter," and be ready to
go forward or to retreat with honor according as the
action of the General Assembly and the final efforts
for the establishment seemed to be favorable or unfavorable. In a letter written after his father had
been some time in New York, guiding the plans and
watching the progress of events, he expressed his
pleasure to learn that the opposing party had not
gained any strength to defeat so excellent a purpose,
and remarked: " With regard, however, to the main
question, — your determining to continue there, —
we are indeed at a loss. For myself, I find I shall be
so much disadvantaged by the removal, that I cannot
heartily assent to it at any rate, much less on any
but the most advantageous and certain terms."

The removal was finally accomplished, and then he
became separated from the immediate companionship
of the paternal household, and only saw its members
at distant intervals, or in the long summer vacation.
It deprived him of the opportunity of those personal
consultations which had been so freely interchanged
between them, and compelled him to the more fre-

quent and cautious use of his pen as a correspondent.
His busy life, as a professional man, did not prevent
him from keeping his father informed of every political event that bore upon the prosperity of his native
colony, and he received in return the freshest intelligence of any civil or ecclesiastical movements in New
York. In this way they mutually aided each other,
and supplied, in a measure, the absence of personal
intercourse.

CHAPTER II.

DEATH OF HIS BROTHER; PROFESSIONAL REPUTATION; CORRE-
SPONDENCE WITH JARED INGERSOLL, COLONIAL AGENT AT
LONDON; WALLINGFORD CONTROVERSY; DESCRIPTION OF
COUNTRY ABOUT LONDON, AND CHARACTER OF WILLIAM PITT.

A. D. 1755–1761.

WILLIAM, his younger brother, was chosen a Tutor in the College at New York, but late in the autumn of 1755 he resigned the office, and in imitation of his father's example, thirty-three years before, embarked for England to receive Holy Orders. His death there, of the small-pox, just as he was on the eve of returning to his native land, was a painful disappointment and affliction to the family, and created stronger bonds of tenderness and solicitude between the father and his surviving son. His father wrote him from New York, on his thirtieth birthday, under the burden of oppressive sorrow for his terrible bereavement, and having blessed God for preserving his two sons so long to him, added : —

"May He preserve you still, and lengthen out to you a useful life to a good old age, and bestow ten thousand blessings on you and yours. And as I always set my heart upon your being, both, great and public blessings to mankind, and now one is taken

away, and some part of your private care is thereby
abated, I trust you will be so much the more of a
public spirit and lay out your life and talents to the
best advantage for public usefulness, and that as
much as you can in what relates to the interest of
religion as well as justice."

The reputation which Mr. Johnson had by this
time attained in his profession, brought him promi-
nently before the public in the trial of the most difficult cases, and among them those which involved
heated religious controversies. In all great legal
troubles or suits, unhappily forced upon Churchmen
in different parts of the Colony, he was sure to be
applied to by them, and secured, if possible, for a
counselor, and the utmost confidence was invaria-
bly reposed in his judgment and candor. Like other
good lawyers of every period in civil history, he was
sometimes on the wrong side and failed to gain his
case. But as the mortification of losing a suit in a
court of justice belongs rather to the client than to
the advocate, neither his business nor his fame suffered on this account. He was an eager student of
English politics and of English literature as well, and
early took a deep interest in the relations of the
American Colonies to the home Government. When
Jared Ingersoll, a friend and contemporary of his, and
afterwards the famous stamp-master, went to England
as an agent for the Colony of Connecticut, he wrote
to Johnson from London three months after his arrival there a long letter, dated April 17, 1759; and
having first given a graphic description of the metropolis, he proceeded to speak of the delightful country
through which he passed for three hundred miles in

his journey from Falmouth to London, "all green
as May; the full blade and leaf of the spear and
clover-grass teeming with vigorous life; the herds
and flocks feeding, and the husbandmen plowing;
no waste grounds unless here and there a heath, and
even that feeding thousands of young cattle and
sheep; all cultivated in the neatest manner, no
sunken swamps, no rocky, stony places; the hill
and the vale equally covered with a rich profusion
of nature's bounty."

After this outburst of admiration for the scenery
of England, he turned to present a picture of what
he knew would greatly interest his friend, and paid
him a high and delicate compliment in the comparison which he made between him and the great English advocates whom it had been his fortune to hear.

You will naturally suppose that I have improved some of
my leisure hours in looking into the several courts; it was
term time when I came; accordingly I attended some little
at the King's Bench, some at Chancery, at the Common
Pleas, and at the sittings at Guildhall, — have also been in
the House of Commons, and have heard argued several causes
on appeal before the House of Lords, and some at the
Cockpit before the Council, etc. The late Lord Chancellor
Hardwick, the present Lord Chief Justice Mansfield, and the
Lord Keeper Henley seem to be very much the Triumvirate
who decide all matters of weight at whatever board. If a
Committee of the Privy Council be appointed to hear any
cause brought by appeal before the King in Council, Hardwick and Mansfield are sure to be two of them, and to have
no inconsiderable hand in the determination. In the House
of Lords, the Lord Keeper brings on no cause of appeal till
Hardwick and Mansfield come, and truly the rest of the
House seem to take but little notice of the arguments; and
as these gentlemen give their opinion, so the cause is deter-

mined. These three personages are great in the law and
't is well no doubt that a deference is paid to their opinion
in law matters. I have heard an Attorney and Solicitor
General, Advocate General of Scotland, and divers others
speak at the Bar of this and 'tother court; many of them
speak *well, and yet, was I not afraid of offending your modesty, I would tell you that I think I have* heard *somebody in
Connecticut speak as well as any of them.*

I have not had the happiness of hearing Mr. Pitt speak
in the House. He made a pretty alarming speech one day
since my arrival; but I was so unhappy as to be unwell that
day. I have conversed with him at his own house. His
manner is agreeable, but nothing very peculiar as to oratory
is collectible, I think, from his private conversation. And
now what shall I say further? If I should undertake to
tell you how his Majesty and the several branches of the
Royal family look, 't would be no very valuable piece of information; besides, you know already as much of that matter
as you can by hearsay. Should I tell you Mr. Garrick is a
very fine actor upon the stage, 't would be no news to you, and
what the political world are about I know no more than you,
and 't is well if they all know what they are about themselves.
May success attend his Majesty's arms in America this campaign. Oh! that peace was again restored to the earth.

To this letter Johnson made an extended reply,
and introduced topics of an exciting public character which centered in New Haven and its vicinity.
It would be a pity to mar his sober view of them by
an imperfect quotation, and therefore the whole of
that part of his reply, which was dated September 10,
1759, is given in this connection. He began thus: —

DEAR SIR, — I now return you my hearty thanks for
your kind favor of April 17, which arrived in July, while I
was in New York; but I had not the pleasure of reading it
till my return home the beginning of August. The letter,

I assure you, gave me great pleasure, both as it acquainted me with your health and welfare, in which I shall always have the utmost satisfaction, but also, as it assured me that you still retain, amidst all the gayeties and brilliancies of London, some remembrance of us. May our friendship and affection still continue unabated and unaltered by any change of place, time, or circumstances. I should have answered your letter before, but the two last packets were hurried away so suddenly with the happy news of our successes, that we had no notice of their sailing, and since, the circuit has taken up most of my time till New Haven court, from whence I returned sick with the measles, of which I am now recovering. Mrs. Ingersoll was the last person I saw in New Haven, who, with your son, was very well. She bears your absence with the patience of a heroine, though I doubt not, as she says, she is extremely desirous of your return and anxious for the happy period when she may greet your return to your native country.

The last thing I did at New Haven court was to lose the cause between Mr. Noyes and the society, for his salary, which you will believe I did not much regret. It is said the New Light Party lose ground and apprehend themselves in danger of becoming the minor party; at least it is certain they are very solicitous for a division of the society, which was argued by them last Assembly, and is to come on again in October; but is rather retarded by Mr. Noyes's party. You will not forget with how much warmth you urged it when we opposed it. The sides seem to be changed, and I, a poor hackney lawyer for bread, am compelled to espouse the cause of parties whose spirit I cannot enter into. But *Tempora mutantur* you know. In all these affairs, however, I endeavor to follow our friend Pope's advice, to retain my native moderation, and only go on as the storm drives.

But why do I mention the religious controversies of New Haven when they are so far distanced by the controversy of Wallingford. This is a most high dispute, and engages

2

the attention of the whole Colony; it took up a great part
of the Assembly's time last session, and I presume will more
of it in October, nothing having yet been done to put an
end to it. What pity it is that you are not here to take
part in this curious dispute (whether the people or the clergy
shall supply the parishes with ministers), that you might
gain a thorough understanding of your ecclesiastical constitution, the deep mysteries of which I doubt you have never
yet looked into. But as the controversy will be in print, I
hope you will not entirely by your absence lose the benefit
of those interesting disquisitions and researches which this
dispute has occasioned; and I trust your friends at New
Haven will also preserve many curious anecdotes to acquaint
you with at your return, as well as for the subject of their
letters to you while you remain in England. Once in my
life, Mr. Darling tells me, I am on the right side, — what he
calls so I need not tell you. But I detain you too long on
a subject which, though it bears the name of religion, I
know you think very ill deserves the name, and is not of
that importance which the zeal of parties would put upon it.

Johnson was grateful for the account given of the
English courts of law, and pleased to have an insight
into the character and influence of the leading Lords
in Council, but he rather playfully turned the
words which put so high an estimate upon his own
eloquence. "Your fine compliment to me," he said,
"would indeed have made me blush had I not been
prepared to impute it to your fondness for the productions of your dear native country, and your too
partial friendship for me, which will not suffer you
to see me in a true light."

The next letter from Mr. Ingersoll contains so
many good things, including a graphic description of
the country about London, as it then appeared, and

of the character of William Pitt, the statesman and orator, that it would not be well presented by extracts. It is dated, —

LONDON, 22 / *December*, 1759.

DEAR SIR, — Your favor of the 10th September came safe to hand the 27th ult. If you knew with how much greediness my eyes devoured every line of what.you are pleased to call a long tedious letter, you would not have made it a syllable shorter than it is. My native country, my native and early friends, have gained too strong hold of my affections to be soon forgotten by me; to hear of their welfare, therefore, must be ever agreeable to me, while detained at this great remove from them. I do assure you, nothing gives me greater pleasure than to think I shall yet again live with my family, and ride with you to Hartford and elsewhere, in the old round of business. It is true I live here very much at ease ; have enough to eat, drink, and wear ; and, thank God, enjoy a good state of health, and have a good appetite to taste these necessary enjoyments, and the other amusements, as well as the more profitable and instructive entertainments of this grand metropolis. Yet I look upon myself as a traveller only. I can cheerfully stay awhile, and with my present temper of mind, after that, can as cheerfully return to my proper home, and be content to live and die among my American friends.

You write me, as do others of my friends, considerable of the religious jars and confusions, yet subsisting at New Haven and Wallingford. I must say to you, as I have to my other friends, if any person be troubled with a disputatious turn of mind in religious matters, let him be sent to London. There is something in the temperament of the air here, at this present day, so efficacious with regard to disorders of that kind, that I dare answer for it nine out of ten, that shall try the experiment, will meet with an effectual cure. You think it a pity I am not at home at this time, to gain an intimate acquaintance with the ecclesiastical condition

of my country; the deep mysteries of which you seem to
suppose I am not altogether master of. You know, sir, that
people troubled with jaundice see all things yellow. I tell
you again, send those yellow-sighted people to London, and
they will see all things agreeably, and nothing out of order.
The parson here who teaches, and the easy congregations
who are taught, to be sure, spy no defect in the blessed constitution hierarchical; and should either happen to discover
any little flaw, I dare answer for it they would have more
discretion than to disturb their neighbors about it. Nor are
the people here in a mood to be disturbed by any such thing.
To be serious, sir, you know my sentiments with regard to
these things very well; that not unfrequently the mighty
bustle made about ecclesiastical constitution, and wrong
steps in ecclesiastical proceedings, are but mere pretexts to
cover what is really at bottom, — pride, envy, malice, insa-
tiable thirst after dominion, superiority, and the like. I
wish to God I may find all those disputes at an end before
my return home; for I do more than ever hate and despise
them.

Your observation on what I wrote you of the soil of this
country, is doubtless very just; that the difference of fertility in different countries is very much owing to the number and industry of the inhabitants. I mentioned to you
the fertility of the grounds round about London. Since I
wrote you I have seen much more of them, and when I
have observed to Mr. Jackson (with whom I have frequently
rode out) the richness of the herbage and produce, he always
insists that the land about London on the north side the
river, more especially, is naturally of a gravelly, barren kind;
and he has shown me many places less improved, — places
dug up, etc., to evince it. Indeed, since I wrote you, I have
had much more opportunity than I had before to observe
the lands in different parts of the kingdom, and in the summer season. I have been through Surrey, Sussex, into Essex,
to Bristol, Bath, and across the Severn into some parts of
Wales, and through many whole counties. I find the lands

different in different parts; nor do I think any of them exceed naturally, if they may compare with, the Hartford and
Wethersfield lands, and perhaps some others in Connecticut.
But when you consider that travel as far as you will, and
where you will, you see no sunken swamps, no stony, unim-
proved lands, nor any barren naked hills or other grounds
(except some heath), every kind of soil improved in the
proper way; the more dry for plowing, thousands of acres
together; all the lower and more moist for mowing; and
the high smooth hills, as in Sussex, having neither tree, stone,
nor fence, — called Downs, that yield a fine dry grass, improved for feeding thousands of sheep; whatever roughness
there was at the beginning, labor and industry have taken
away. When you consider this, I say, and that nothing is
left undone in point of tillage and manure that can be done,
or that could have been devised as best to be done, through
so many hundreds of years, you will think that England is,
as it really is, a very garden. Such, however, as I doubt
not the western world will be ere long. And oh! that instead of knocking one another in the head, ye were employing your hands to that more valuable purpose, in that infant,
large, and fine country. Of these things I hope to tell you
much more when I have the pleasure to see your face again.

You seem desirous of some particular account of the
characters of the more distinguished personages here, and
of Mr. Pitt in particular. To oblige you I will undertake,
according to my best information and knowledge of that
good man, to draw his picture somewhat minutely, being
confident he would forgive me if he knew it.

As to his person, he is tall, rather slender than corpu-
lent, not quite straight, but bending forward a little about
the shoulders and head; a thin face somewhat pale; a Roman nose; his legs pretty small, and almost all the way of
a bigness, — his ankles being swelled with the gout, which
makes him rather hobble than walk when he goes. His
elocution is good, his voice clear, soft, and masculine. He
delivers himself in the House, in public, in a manner distinct

and forcible.   If he has any fault I think it is in his language being a little too much swollen; seeming to border on
bombast and fustian.   I use harsh words to convey my meaning the better.   You are to remember I say *seeming* to border on that style.   One is afraid as he goes along that he
will fall into that style; though I cannot say that he does.
However, every one has a taste in these things.   He makes
use of a great many very brilliant and striking expressions,
which, being attended with an air and manner sage and
awful as a Cato, make a deep impression on the hearers;
and he may be truly said to be a great orator.   I know
for myself, I have heard him a good many half hours, and
thought them short ones; at the same time I believe he is a
greater speaker than reasoner; and some will have it that
he is not most acquainted with the political state of Europe.
Of that I can say nothing.   In his temper and principles he
is open and determined, polite and easy, with plainness in
ordinary conversation; yet rather blunt than soothing to
persons who he thinks are not acting from truly patriotic
principles.   This, some think a fault; and that by that
means he needlessly offends some persons who may have it
in their power to do mischief.   However, as to this particular, there are different opinions.   If he alters his own opinion
in any political matter, he is the first to tell it without any
kind of hiding.   I have heard him own in terms in the
House, that he had altered his opinion in some measure from
what it formerly was, with regard to *Continental Measures.*
That he despises money is most certain; which gives occasion for his enemies to say he is lavish enough with the
nation's money.   Nor is he at all fond of pomp and show.
He is obliged indeed to keep up something of it as a Secretary of State, but is never so happy when free from business as when with his family.   I do not believe him insen-
sible to the charms of honors; but I have great reason to
believe that his greatest pride, or ambition, is in deserving
well of his King and country; and in receiving the just
plaudits of the same.   In a most charming speech he made

the first day of the session of Parliament, taking notice of some compliments that had been made by other gentlemen who spoke in the House before him, he said : —

"If in anything I have contributed to the service of my country, I rejoice. My worthy friend who spoke last, was pleased to pay my services a high compliment, which I impute to the partiality of that friendship with which he has been pleased to honor me. I will own I have a zeal to serve my country, and that beyond what the weakness of my frail body admits of. I hope I am in no danger of having my vanity flattered by any successes, or by any compliments made me in consequence. I am sure I think there is no room for it, when I consider how much the events of war depend on what the world calls chance, — a conjunction of incidents which man, short-sighted man, cannot foresee, nor provide against. And when I consider, as I have every day considered since your recess from Parliament, that it is uncertain whether the day shall end in acclamations of joy for good news received, or whether I shall fall a sacrifice to the fury of an enraged multitude, on account of some notable disaster happening to the system of the war, which the world is always ready enough to impute to the want of ability, or faithfulness in those that more immediately assist his Majesty," etc., etc., etc.

In a word, he is a great and good man, and has doubtless from his character, principles, and manner had a very great and happy influence on the conduct and behavior of all ranks of men in the several departments of the war.

I find I must break off, as my letter has swelled almost to a volume. As to news it is needless to write you, as you have the whole in public papers. I congratulate you most heartily on the successes in America and here, and hope peace will be the result. There is much talk of a peace, but I can say nothing with certainty about it. Be so good as to call and see my little flock every time you go to New Haven. Remember me to Mrs. Johnson, Mr. Walker and family, and everybody who thinks of me or cares for me.

I will send you a new court calendar as soon as they come
out. I have taken a house very near Westminster Hall,
where I spend much of my time in the several courts of law
and legislation. I take minutes, which I afterwards form
into something like reports. I don't know but you may see
Ingersoll's Reports on the same shelf with Lord Coke's
before you die.

I want to see you that I may prattle a thousand such
foolish things with you. No more, but that I remain your
sincere friend and very humble servant,

JARED INGERSOLL.

The correspondence between them was continued
during Mr. Ingersoll's stay in London. In a letter
dated November 8, 1759, Johnson acquainted him
with events which have become memorable in history, and which are alluded to in the foregoing.
"When I wrote you last, we were in doubt whether
General Wolfe would be able to take Quebec this
fall; but before this or perhaps even that letter
comes to hand, you will have heard of the immortal
honor which that General acquired on the Plains of
Abraham, though with the loss of his life; and of
the surrender of that important capital. There
wanted but a little longer time to have completed
the conquest of Canada, which will be easily effected
in another campaign, if the ministry think fit to continue the war. General Amherst is also returned
from his expedition on Lake Champlain, having de-
stroyed almost all the marine strength of the enemy
there, and secured to himself the fine navigation of
that Lake which is of the utmost importance, — but
it seems the severity of the weather would not permit him to proceed farther. The campaign, which

has proved a most glorious one in America, is now ended, and the troops are returning into winter-quarters.

"Our General Assembly is also just now dissolved, whose resolves, so far as they relate to your agency, you will be acquainted with by his honor. I shall therefore only acquaint you that New Haven and Windsor are at last divided. New Haven on a plan pretty agreeable."

The answer to this letter went largely into a scene of "pretty high complimenting" in the House of Commons, of which Ingersoll was an eye-witness, and wherein one of the Commissioners of the Admiralty and Mr. Charles Townshend figured, making the recent triumph of the British arms in Scotland and Ireland, and the capitulation at Quebec, the text and subject of their encomiums on individual prowess and the militia system in England. "The House," said he, "was quite thrown into an acclamation of joy, and triumph; it is right it should be so; praise is the just reward of military virtue; to be sure we have done brave things lately, and seem to be, as to ourselves, almost ready to leave off, as having conquered enough, — but alas! though we are nearly out of the wood, I don't know how long we must tarry for our friend and ally the King of Prussia. However, we will hope for the best and await the event." And then glancing back to court proceedings in his own colony, he added, —

"I am glad to find that the weapons of war are at last taken from the contending powers at New Haven and Windsor. Amen and Amen. Wallingford, it seems, and the King of Prussia, must fight a

little longer. I wish they may both very soon meet
with a happy issue of all their distresses. And do
Jones and Cooke yet stand side by side in the docket
of controversy? Methinks they fight after they are
dead. I thought they, that is their cause, had spent
the very last breath before I came away; well, if
they love to fight, for fighting sake, let them fight
on, I say; they have money enough, and I am very
sure that out of the much they spend, my good
friend will have a little. Everybody must be about
something. The great Mr. P. and Marshall Belish
are striving which shall get most Indian land in
America, and Mr. Jones and Mr. Cooke are contending which shall have most of good Mr. Cresswell's
old tenor."

CHAPTER III.

CHOSEN MEMBER OF GENERAL ASSEMBLY; INOCULATION FOR
SMALL-POX; PASSAGE OF THE STAMP ACT, AND ARRIVAL OF
JARED INGERSOLL STAMP-MASTER OF CONNECTICUT; ACTION
OF COLONIAL LEGISLATURES; FIRST CONGRESS AT NEW YORK;
REMONSTRANCES TO THE KING AND PARLIAMENT; LETTER OF
JAMES OTIS, AND REPEAL OF THE STAMP ACT.

A. D. 1761–1765.

IN 1761 Mr. Johnson was chosen to represent the
town of Stratford in the Lower House of the General Assembly at its May session, and again he was
elected to represent it at both the May and October
sessions of 1765. That year he was first put in
nomination as an Assistant, and took his seat in the
Upper House at a time when wise and prudent and
learned men were especially needed to temper the
public mind, and infuse into legislative councils a
cautious spirit. Previous to this, however, he had
yielded to the wish often expressed to him by his
father, that he would consent to be inoculated for
the small-pox, that he might escape a disease to
which, in his various journeys, he was liable, and
which had already brought great sorrow to the family. This was before vaccination had been discovered
by Edward Jenner, and applied by the medical pro-

fession as a preventive. Accordingly he went to New
York with a friend, and placed himself under the care
of a physician, who was giving his special attention
to treatment by inoculation; and with the Divine
blessing, he was carried safely through the peril, and
returned in good health to his household. Soon after
reaching New York, he wrote to his father the following letter, dated April 2, 1764; which, besides speaking of his own "affair," gives other information that
is valuable in history : —

HONORED SIR, — You will see by the papers, that the
Packet is arrived with two mails, as well as two other London ships; but I do not find they have brought any very
material news, except that of the expulsion of Wilkes, and
his retiring into France. I have looked over several London
papers, and see nothing worth communicating, only that it
is said on the 16th of January, the Archbishop was still at
Dr. Seckers, at Canterbury (where he had been to depose an
offending clergyman), confined by the gout. Several gentlemen have mentioned to me a report as coming by the Packet,
that Connecticut is to be divided between New York and the
Massachusetts Bay; but I cannot discover any good foundation for the story. General Gage is confirmed in his command, and is pushing forward an expedition against the
Indians, under the command of Colonel Broadstreet. Mr.
Cutting was to come with Davis, but could not finish his
affairs soon enough. He is expected in Jacobson, who was
to sail five days after. Captain Hopkins has safely arrived
in England, but I yet hear nothing of Hubbard, etc. I hear
you have letters, but cannot yet come at them. A French
clergyman and a Dutch-English minister came in the
Packet, and the Dutch congregation express great joy at
the arrival of the latter. Mr. Watts has made me a very
friendly visit, inquired very kindly after you (as does everybody I have seen), and desired me to send very freely to

him for anything I may have occasion for. He tells me, by a letter from their agent, it appears very probable that all the colonies will be prohibited (as Connecticut and Massachusetts already are) from making any paper bills a tender, in private payments, at which they are much chagrined. Dr. Barclay was here last Saturday, though very illy able to go abroad ; he looks miserably, and I very much fear his constitution is ruined. His physicians have recommended riding on horseback to him ; if that or something else does not put him in a better state this spring, I think he must give up. He has a letter from Dr. Smith,[1] from Ireland, who has been very ill, — ten weeks confined to his bed, and intends soon to return to America, and leave Sir James[2] to take care of the affairs of the colleges.

They were dissuaded from setting on foot any subscription in Ireland, on account of the heavy losses the people have sustained by the excessive rains and floods ; but were advised to apply to Parliament, which they concluded to do, and to that purpose had engaged the assistance and friendship of the Primate, and other great personages. The collections in England had been returned, to the amount of £5,000 for each college, and it was thought in the whole would turn out about £6,000.

Mr. Cooper has also been unwell, but is recovering ; and says he intends to make a visit this spring and once a year, as long as he and you live. On this account you will be so good as to let me know before I return how your port wine holds out, that if there should be occasion, I may send you a fresh supply. Mr. Stuyvesant is very well, and as usual very friendly ; he supplies me with milk, on which I live almost entirely.

No opportunity has yet offered to say anything of your affair, or of my own projects, as I have hitherto seen all our friends only in mixed company ; and I dare say when-

---

[1] Rev. William Smith, D. D., soliciting funds for the College at Philadelphia.

[2] Sir James Jay, for the College in New York.

ever I do mention them, it will be to little purpose, as they
seem all to be so engrossed by their own plans of private
pleasure or profit, as to have very little time left to attend
to anything else. I am very glad to see by yours to Mr.
Auchmuty, that you are all well. As to our particular affair, we have been every day taking medicine of one kind or
other, and this morning took physic. To-morrow the doctor proposes to inoculate us. He desires his compliments to
you, and says everything has hitherto operated as he could
wish. Meantime I am very calm and easy about the affair,
have good spirits, and doubt not, by the blessing of God,
shall pass safely through the distemper. I am much more
concerned for you and my dear wife than for myself ; but
hope you will not be anxious. I don't know whether it will
be safe for me to write after inoculation ; if not shall get
somebody else to let you know how we are.

The news of the passage of the Stamp Act had
reached America, and the Connecticut stamp-master,
Jared Ingersoll, who had been a second time in England, had already arrived, and been met with violent
and insulting opposition in the attempt to execute
the duties of his office. It was a vastly disquieting
measure, and the popular ferments spread in every
direction. Mr. Ingersoll, who did not resign as soon
as he saw the temper of the country, addressed
the General Assembly, convened at Hartford by
special order of the Governor, and, after briefly
reciting the history of the act, expressed the hope
that tumults would be avoided, and the people of the
Colony saved from going into any violent measures.
But his address availed nothing towards allaying the
popular uneasiness. It was followed by extraordinary resistance, and a declaration was extorted from
him to renounce the office of stamp-master, — an

office which, he frankly informed the Board of Commissioners at home, was "at that time the most odious of anything that can well be imagined. I have found myself," he continued, "in the most distressed situation between the obligations of my office and the resentments of the people ; but hope it will not be long before I shall be rid of both."[1]

The Colonial legislatures took up the matter, and hoping that England would have more respect for the opposition and remonstrances of a united body, than for the complaints of private individuals, they accepted a proposition, first suggested by James Otis, of Massachusetts, to hold a Congress of all the Colonies, — a Congress which should consist of commissioners or committees, appointed by the several General Assemblies, and consult together about the best method of allaying the popular excitement, and seeking relief from various acts of the British Parliament.

This Congress was appointed to meet at New York, on the first Tuesday of October, 1765, which was the first day of the month, and twenty-seven commissioners from nine of the thirteen Colonies were present ; Georgia, North Carolina, Virginia, and New Hampshire not being represented. Johnson, with Eliphalet Dyer and David Rowland, appeared for Connecticut ; and the proceedings, which were not hurriedly entered upon, lasted till three o'clock in the afternoon of the 25th, when the Congress broke up, and the members returned to their homes. It was a body of men that assembled to state the grievances of the Colonies, and not to give utterance to any sentiments of disloyalty to the King and the English Government.

---

[1] Ingersoll's *Letters*, p. 55.

The Stamp Act was a measure of Grenville, the minister, who, after the close of the war with France, in 1763, conceived the idea that the Americans ought to support themselves; and that being colonial subjects, and not free Britons, it was perfectly proper to impose duties upon them, to obtain a revenue without allowing them the privilege of a hearing or representation in Parliament. Chatham, Colonel Barre, and General Conway in vain opposed the measure, and its adoption and enforcement led the Colonists to examine their situation, and finding that they were not deserters from England, or transported for any fault or crime, but that all the settlements were made under express charters from the crown, and by consent of the government, they claimed to be British subjects, and to be entitled, under the rights, liberties, and laws of England, to every privilege enjoyed by them in the old country. It was upon these conclusions that the proceedings and resolves of the Congress were based, and the tax declared to be illegal.

Johnson concurred in all, and was a guiding and controlling spirit in the Assembly. He drew up the petitions, and remonstrances to the King and two Houses of Parliament, which the President, Timothy Ruggles, of Massachusetts, refused to sign. This was kept a profound secret, as he could not have returned home through New England in safety had the fact become known. The commissioners or delegates reported their doings to the several Colonial Legislatures, and in Connecticut the thought was entertained of sending a special agent to London with the documents, and Johnson was named as a suitable person to be intrusted with the duty. A letter to him from James Otis, dated at Boston, November 12, 1765, refers to this; and as it has never been published entire, and is otherwise interesting as showing the spirit of the times, it may be well to produce it just as it was written : —

DEAR SIR, — I received yours, and am very glad to find your Assembly so far approving of the measures taken at the Congress. I could have wished they had sent an agent from among them. I had the pleasure, as I came through the Colony, to hear you named as a candidate. The Assembly here have done us the honor fully to approve of our proceedings, and have voted the thanks of the House to their Committee. There was a motion to except the Briga dier, our notable President; but as he was absent, I apolo gized for his strange conduct as well as I could, and the proposed discrimination subsided. The people of this Province, however, will never forgive him.

We are much surprised at the violent proceedings at New York, as there has been so much time for people to cool, and the outrages on private property are so generally detested. By a vessel from South Carolina, we learn that the people were in a tumult at Charleston, and terrible consequences apprehended. God knows what all these things will end in, and to Him they must be submitted. In the mean time, 'tis much to be feared the Parliament will charge the Colonies with presenting petitions in one hand, and a dagger in the other. Pray for the peace of Jerusalem, as I do for your prosperity, and am much your friend and humble servant,

J. OTIS.

The petitions and remonstances of this Congress, the continued resistance and disorders in America, and the troubles and commotions in England combined to make the juncture a critical one for the government. Grenville was at length dismissed, and a new ministry was formed, with the Marquis of

Rockingham as the first Lord of the Treasury, and
Conway, a zealous friend to the American cause, as
Secretary of State for the Colonies.   In just one year
after its passage, the Stamp Act[1] was repealed ; and
the Governor and Company of the Colony of Connecticut sent an address to the King, penned again
by Johnson, " returning their most grateful tribute
of humble and hearty thanks to his Majesty," for the
favor, and among other things thus reciting in courtly
phrase : " The unshaken loyalty of this Colony, and
their warm devotion to your Majesty, and your glorious progenitors of the illustrious House of Hano-
ver, have ever been the boast of this Colony.   Under
their auspicious protection, we have enjoyed in their
full extent those rights and liberties granted by your
Royal progenitors, and established upon the public
faith, — which, from small beginnings, have, under
God, been the means of rendering this Colony a
valuable part of your Majesty's dominions ; and as
your Majesty's gracious condescension, upon the late
most important and interesting occasion, must in the
strongest manner engage the hearts and affections of
all your subjects to your Majesty, so we beg leave
to assure your Majesty that we think ourselves bound
by the strongest ties of religion, loyalty, and gratitude, to make all the dutiful returns that can be paid
by the most obedient subjects to the best and most
indulgent Sovereign.'

[1] Appendix A.

CHAPTER IV.

A. D. 1765–1767.

In February, 1766, Connecticut was cited to appear
before the King and Lords in Council, to answer in a
matter which had been kept in agitation for nearly
seventy years, and concerned the title to a large
tract of land that Lieutenant Governor Mason was
appointed to obtain for the Colony, from the Mohegan Indians. He took the deed to himself, and the
fact remained unnoticed until after his death ; when
the property was claimed by his heirs for services
rendered to the Indians, as their agent. It was a
part of their suit, too, to oppose the claim of Connecticut under pretense of protecting the rights of the
Indians ; and they appealed from the legal decisions
against them in this country to the highest tribunal
in England : while the title to the land was valuable,
the most important question was one which affected
the chartered rights of the Colony ; for had they succeeded, " the conduct of Mason would have been
adjudged fraudulent, and the British Government

would have made it a ground for taking away the charter."

Dr. Johnson — for by this time the University of Oxford had honored him with the degree of Doctor of Laws [1] — was appointed by the General Assembly, at its October Session, 1766, to proceed to England, and defend in that cause. The time for appearance was short ; but wishing to be personally informed respecting the Indians, he went to Mohegan himself, and with the aid of the Governor and Lieutenant Governor called a council of them, and after careful inquiry into their circumstances and condition, found them contented and happy, with no complaints to raise against the government of the Colony. Repairing to New York, he went on board the Halifax packet the day before Christmas, and after a boisterous voyage, arrived at Falmouth, and reached London on the 8th of February, in season to enter his appearance before the Lords in Council, prior to the day assigned. As he had been directed to do by the General Assembly, he consulted Richard Jackson, the colony's resident agent, prepared the case for trial, and notified Mason, the representative of the claimants, that he was ready for the hearing. But then Mason declared that he was unprepared, and must have time to send to New England for further evidence ; and as it was a court without terms, sitting only when business was pressing, and the law lords would attend, Johnson had no means of compelling him to a trial, and was, therefore, by various delays and postponements, detained in England far beyond the limit he had expected to be absent.

[1] It was conferred January 23d, 1766.

The following is the first long letter which he wrote to his father after his arrival, and after he had obtained some knowledge of the views and policy of leading statesmen, in regard to American affairs. It was a time when vigorous efforts were in progress to secure the consecration of Bishops for this country, and he quietly used his influence in this direction, but gave his father little or no hope of immediate success, and cautioned him against making public his letters, especially when he took the liberty to mention names, and even private conversations.

LONDON, *April* 4th, 1767.

HONORED SIR, — I have the inexpressible pleasure to find by yours of the 11th of February, that you and my family were then all well, as I have the satisfaction to inform you I have been myself ever since I left you. I hope long before this time you have received my first letter, acquainting you with the very boisterous passage we had to Falmouth, and of my safe arrival here.

Nothing very material, either with regard to the public or myself, has occurred since my last, of the 6th and 10th of March, to you, and of the 14th to my wife. The Ministry patched up a temporary peace amongst themselves about that time, and have continued since, tolerably, to save appearances; but from every circumstance it appears that the friendship is not very sincere, and that there is little cordial harmony amongst them; so that a change is much talked of, and by some confidently expected. Lord Chatham and Lord Shelburne are together; the Duke of Grafton and Secretary Conway are pretty well agreed; but do not, it is said, altogether approve of the designs of the two first, and Charles Townshend will be directed by none of them, and is beside so unsteady that he has no fixed plan of his own. The East India affair has taken up all the time of the House of Commons, and is yet as undetermined and uncertain as ever. The 30th and 31st of March, I was present at two very warm debates, in the House of Lords, on American affairs, particularly the refusal of New York to billet the troops, in which the Duke of Richmond, Earls Temple, Talbot, Sandwich, Suffolk, and Lords Lyttleton, Weymouth, Ravensworth, etc., were very severe upon the Colonies, and those lords who last year denied the right of Parliament to tax the Colonies. The Lord Chancellor, the Duke of Grafton, and Lord Shelburne endeavored to defend their former opinions, and to soften the resentments against the Colonies, though they would not attempt to excuse the conduct of New York. They all seemed zealous enough to do something effectual upon this occasion, but were by no means agreed what course to take, and there is some reason to imagine that the difficulties they will meet with, when they set down in earnest to form any plan, will be too many to be got over during the remainder of this session.

There is no great danger, I believe, of their meddling with our Charters at present, and you will see by my last that nothing is like to be done while I am here, relating to the affair you mention, so that my countrymen (if they are any of them jealous of me), may make themselves easy as to any mischief they may imagine I might do them; and I wish I may find it in my power, as much as I am sure it is in my inclination, to do them some service.

I can make no guess yet when the Mohegan case will come on. We have preferred a petition for the New Hampshire Lands, upon which I have had several audiences of Lord Shelburne, the principal manager of American affairs, who speaks very favorably upon the subject. The Society have also petitioned for a confirmation of their rights, and done me the honor to appoint me their agent in that affair; so that I have business enough in hand to prevent my acquiring any habits of idleness while I am in England.

Some time since I happily met the Bishop of Oxford at Dr. Burton's, and seized the opportunity to give him your and my own thanks for his Prelections, with which he was certainly not displeased. As you desired me, I went into a conversation with him on the study of Hebrew. He has never seen Parkhurst's Lexicon, and could tell me nothing about it, and thinks Taylor's Concordance and Lexicon the best, — which, by the way, I will get for you if you would like to have it. When I inquired about the state of the Hutchinsonians, he replied, that whim is very much declining, and going out of vogue, and seemed to think that Dr. Sharpe had sufficiently answered them in those points which he undertook ; but upon the whole I thought he had not very much attended to those matters, nor made any particular examination of the Hutchinsonian principles. He was so kind as to ask me to come and see him, which I did very soon, when he entered into a conversation on the state of religion, etc., both in this country and in America, which fully confirmed me in the opinion which I had before conceived, that in this country there is not much religion amongst the highest and lowest ranks of people, though I hope there is a good deal among the middling sort. The King, the Bishops to a man, and the worthy serious part of the people, were, he said, enough disposed to do everything that could be wished for the interest of religion in America. But the great people, and the Ministry, whatever party prevailed, would give no attention to subjects of that kind, partly because they hardly think them worth their attention, having been so long neglected, but especially because the different parties are so continually opposing, persecuting, and perplexing each other, that those in power have always enough to do to keep themselves in place, and in any tolerable manner get along with those affairs which are absolutely necessary to be done. Add to this that the changes have of late been so frequent, that if they were ever so well inclined, they were removed before they could have time to digest and execute any plan of importance.

His Lordship is as polite and affable as he is learned. When I mentioned his controversy with the Bishop of Gloucester, he answered, it was not a controversy, but an idle squabble, which his Lordship of Gloucester had drawn

him into, and which he was very willing to forget. Since
you are pleased, said he, to take notice of my Lectures in
America, I will send you a dozen of my larger confutation
of Bishop Hare, for your father, Dr. Auchmuty, Dr. Cooper,
Dr. Chandler, and such as you think they may be agreeable
to. They are not yet come to hand, but I dare say he will
not forget to send them in due time.

I have not seen his Grace since I wrote you, but intend to
wait upon him ere long. I have already acquainted you that
I had informed him of what you had written me relating
to the Indian schools, and that I doubt not he has taken in
very good part all you have said to him.

I am much obliged to Mr. Harrison for his kind letter, and
intentions to recommend me to Sir George Savile, with whom
I should gladly enough be acquainted, though I have already
more acquaintances than I very well know how to attend to,
and find it not very difficult to make others, as I may have
occasion. If I go into the North I will certainly make a
visit to Mrs. Bell, and hope I shall be able to find some
traces of the relation which you imagine subsists between us.

I am much obliged to Mr. Chapman for his kindness and
assistance to my family, and beg he will accept my particular thanks ; and with compliments to him and to all friends,
and tenderest love to my wife and children, I remain, Honored Sir, your most dutiful son and humble servant,

WM. SAMUEL JOHNSON.

Dr. Johnson became somewhat impatient, and, according to the entries in his Diary, made frequent
visits to Richard Jackson, to consult with him and
others upon the Mohegan case. But still the hearing
was delayed, and the business of his special agency
could not be accomplished. On Friday, the 17th of
April, he "set out at four o'clock, with Temple[1] and
Palmer, for Cambridge," and was absent from Lon-

[1] Appendix B.

don ten days, spending Easter at the seat of that venerable University, and making himself acquainted with Heads of Colleges, and objects of interest.

One of the most exciting and important debates on American affairs that ever took place in Parliament was entered upon immediately after his return to the metropolis. Irritating resolutions were proposed in the House on the 15th of May, and after an eloquent advocacy by Townshend, adopted without a division. These were followed by other severe measures, and Grenville, in one of his impassioned speeches, looking up to the gallery of spectators, said, " I hope there are no American agents present; I must hold such language as I would not have them hear." And yet Johnson dared to sit there, at the risk of being arrested and imprisoned, and to take down the words of the debaters and transmit them to his friends in Connecticut.

It should be mentioned here that Grenville and his political connections were hostile to America, and he took every opportunity in Parliament to say harsh things about the Colonies, and to complain of his dismission from the ministry, and the repeal of the Stamp Act. He was indirectly the promoter, if not the cause of the second class of taxation, which finally became the ground of the Revolution. According to Johnson, who carefully noted the drift of Parliamentary measures, this second taxation originated in a peculiar and unexpected manner. Lord Chatham was Prime Minister at the time, and as is well known. opposed to raising a revenue in America by the imposition of duties ; but unfortunately, at the opening of Parliament (1767), he was seized with a fit of the gout, and went down to Bath, and was confined there and at Marlborough during the whole session. The leadership in the House of Commons was intrusted in his absence to Charles Townshend, one of the Ministry, a young man of fine talents, and an able speaker and manager, — but full of fire and frequently off his guard. Whether designedly or not is uncertain; but Grenville took advantage of his impulsiveness, and one evening when he was declaiming as usual on American affairs, he went so far as to say, addressing himself to the minister, "You are cowards; you are afraid of America," repeating the taunt in different language, upon which Townshend took fire, rose and said, "Fear, fear, cowards, dare not tax America. I dare tax America." For a few moments Grenville stood silent and then said, "Dare you tax America? I wish to God I could see it." And Townshend replied, "I will, I will."

"Next morning," relates Johnson in his narrative, "I knew from an American and member of Parliament, — a friend of Townshend, with whom he and others had supped, — that at supper he said, 'I have done a very foolish thing to-night, which Mr. Grenville's impetuosity has driven me into, to promise to tax America. I love America, and don't wish to harass them; but cannot you, gentlemen, tell me of some paltry tax to impose, by which I can get out of the scrape, and stop the mouths of these wrangling disputants.'" And so the tax upon tea was afterwards levied, as being least calculated to be disagreeable to the American people. But how little had British statesmen comprehended the true principle which lay at the bottom of the whole controversy! It was not the quantity or the quality of the tax — whether it was burdensome or light — that concerned the Colonies. They denied the right of England to lay any tax at all upon them, and Grenville's great argument, which he was perpetually enforcing in Parliament, and which the friends of America were least able to answer or oppose, was that the late war, known by us in history as the old French War, had been undertaken at the request of the Colonies, and solely for their benefit; that, though successful in removing from them an enemy of whom they had been greatly in fear, and by whom they had been much perplexed, it had been attended with an immense expense; and that, therefore, they ought to bear a part of it, as well as to take upon themselves to provide in some degree for the support of their own provincial governments.

Among other letters to his countrymen, giving an account of Parliamentary proceedings, Johnson wrote to his father from London, May 18th, 1767, as follows : —

HONORED SIR, — We have been for some time in anxious expectation of the Parliamentary discussion of American affairs, which has been repeatedly postponed till last Wednesday; when the Chancellor of the Exchequer, in a Committee of the whole House, opened the plan, which consists of these particulars : An Act of Parliament to disfranchise New York, or in other words, disable them from making any laws whatever, till they submit to the late Act of Parliament for quartering soldiers : To establish a Board of Commissioners of Customs in America, similar to that here, in order the better to prevent smuggling : To impose taxes upon paper, window-glass, china ware, white lead, and painters' colors, upon wine, oil, lemons, and raisins from

Portugal, and permit American ships to proceed directly
from thence to the Colonies: And to render the governors
and judges in the king's governments independent of the
people, by establishing their salaries, the first at £2,000,
and the latter at £500 per annum, to be paid out of the American revenue. The first of these is already passed, and most
of the others will probably be come into. Several of these
regulations, especially that with respect to New York and
the independency of the governors, will no doubt be thought,
as indeed they are, very severe, and will probably widen the
breach between this country and that; but at present all objections are disregarded; the spirit is warm against America,
and they seem resolved to enforce obedience to the Legislature of this country, and bring the Colonies to what they
esteem a proper state of obedience. Mr. Grenville, among
other things, proposed a political test for America, that no
person should be allowed to sit in any assembly or exercise
any office in the Plantations without first subscribing a Declaration, nearly in the words of the late Declaratory Act of
Parliament, acknowledging the sovereignty of this country,
and the right of Parliament to tax America.

The spirit is greatly changed with respect to America:
last year they were all for favoring and relieving us; now
they are as much engaged to lay burdens upon us, and reduce us to subjection. So unstable are the counsels of the
nation! They do not choose to attack us all at once, lest the
Colonies should again unite, and it was for some time a doubt
which to take first, New York or Massachusetts Bay; but as
the disobedience of the first was the most direct, they concluded to begin with that Province, and she is to serve for
an example to the other Colonies, who, they imagine, not
being attacked, will take no part in the dispute.

On Friday, the report of the Committee being made to
the House, a motion was made for re-committing the resolutions relating to New York; but after a long debate it was
approved. Mr. Grenville then moved his Test above mentioned, which, after a further warm debate, he lost — 43 to

146. After this he said, since he saw the House would not come into any effectual resolutions in support of their own sovereignty and authority, he hoped they would at least do something for those who had endeavored to support it in America, and had suffered in consequence of their obedience to the Acts of this Legislature, meaning the Stamp Act; he therefore moved that an humble address should be presented to his Majesty, that he would be pleased to bestow some marks of his favor upon those governors and officers in America who had suffered by their loyalty, etc.; in which all parties concurred with him, and it was carried, *nemine contradicente*. He also moved for some Parliamentary favors to the Island of Barbadoes, for their distinguished loyalty, but this was rejected. Thus you see there is at present neither inclination nor opportunity to provide for any Americans except those who incurred the resentment of the people of that country, by their conduct relative to the Stamp Act. The Chief Justiceship of New York is thought of for Mr. Ingersoll, but it may be best not to mention this at present, as it is not yet known whether the engagement which had been made of it to another person (I imagine Mr. Gardiner) can be decently avoided, but he and the other sufferers will certainly have the first things that offer.

Upon looking into the papers relating to the dispute between the Governors of the College of New York, and Sir James Jay, in which they have desired me to assist Mr. Trecothick, I find, as I apprehended, that Sir James intends to make use of the letters he has obtained from you, and of your evidence against the College. They insist that he offered his service to them. He says you first applied to him in behalf of the College, and persuaded him to undertake the affair. They say (and so is the Report of the Committee under your hand, you being one of them) that he was to have such an allowance for his trouble, etc., as *they* should judge reasonable. He insists (and founds himself upon your letter) that they were not to judge of the reward, but that it was to be generous and honorable, and therefore demands

a guinea per day for his expenses, and the like sum for his
services for two years, amounting to above £1,500 sterling.
It is possible the matter may be accommodated (which I
shall labor to effect very sincerely), but in case it should not,
your evidence will no doubt be called for; certainly by Sir
James, and very probably by the College. I do not indeed
imagine that what he has from you already will greatly serve
him; but I mention it to you now, that you may be upon
your guard, and write nothing farther to either party, nor
give any evidence but in a regular way, and after an examination of the Report of the Committee, which you signed,
and the copies of the letters which you have written, which, I
shall insist with Sir James if he moves for a commission to
examine you, that you shall be furnished with.

A change of Ministry is still expected, but it is uncertain
when it will take place, or who will turn up. Lord Chatham is quite disabled from public business, and it is even
believed that his understanding is impaired. The East India
affair, which has been all winter in agitation, is yet unsettled,
and a very late session of Parliament is expected. You
see by my last to my wife, that I have been at Cambridge,
and was highly pleased with that University. I intend to
go to Oxford as soon as Parliament rises, which I hope may
be some time in June. I promised myself the pleasure of
letters from you by the Packet which arrived last week; but
am disappointed, and impatient to know how you all do.
Blessed be God, I enjoy perfect health, and with tenderest
love to my wife and the children, and compliments to all
friends, I remain,

Honored Sir, your most dutiful son and humble servant,

WM. SAMUEL JOHNSON.

Mr. Ingersoll, to whom he wrote under the same
date, informing him of the proceedings in Parliament,
replied on the 23d of July, and expressed his surprise
and pleasure that he should be the object of Parliamentary attention, and added: "I am very sensible

of my being indebted for this favor very much to
the assiduous friendship and goodness of Mr. Whately,
as it happens I had written him and you from New
York, where I happened to be in the beginning of
May, with regard to any royal favor that might be
intended for me. I will frame no objections to the
Chief Justiceship of New York, if obtainable, nor to
a seat at the new Board of Revenue, nor to any other
that you shall approve of, as I still have a full confidence both in your judgment and friendship, of which,
indeed, Mr. Whately is pleased to give me new and
fresh proofs in his letter that came with yours." He
was a keen observer of political events, and said to
Johnson : " You must have been in a pretty particular
situation when surreptitiously in the House, hearing
Master Grenville declaim. I hope he said nothing
worse than bad about us ; New York, we understand,
has complied with the Billetting Act. So has escaped
the intended blow."

When the time appointed for the first hearing of
the Mohegan case had arrived, Johnson was well prepared to appear before the Lords in Council. He
knew his position. It was a novel thing for an
American lawyer to plead in so high a court, and
some curiosity was awakened to see how he would
acquit himself. The Lords and Statesmen who heard
him were not only astonished but charmed by his
eloquence, and the impression which he made and
the knowledge he displayed, gained him friends
among the most cultivated minds of the British
realm. An idea may be formed of the simple power
of his oratory, by citing here, though a little in anticipation of the order of events, an anecdote which

is told of him when engaged in the trial of the famous Susquehanna case. That was an old controversy between Connecticut and Pennsylvania about
the jurisdiction of the valley of Wyoming, and late
in the autumn of 1782, Commissioners acting under
the appointment of the Congress of the United
States met at Trenton, to hear the parties in interest, and finally determine the question of proprietorship. Dr. Johnson was one of the three agents for
Connecticut, and the opposing counsel, in the course
of his argument, had read some ancient writing,
recorded on a long roll of parchment, which was
strangely interlarded with passages of Scripture, and
with which he made the Commissioners merry and
jocose by denominating them puritanical fantasy.
When Johnson rose to reply, he was slightly embarrassed, as appeared by his frequent coughing and
expectoration; but soon recovering himself, and
feeling the sting of the reflection upon his native
State conveyed in the words puritanical fantasy, he
seized the parchment, and reading with his silvery
voice and in a tone of marked solemnity the same
passages, he infused an awe into the whole audience;
and then suddenly dropping it, and lifting his hands
and eyes to heaven, he exclaimed, " Great God! is
all this fantasy!" That moment the parchment, dismissed from his hands, rolled as by a spontaneous impulse to his feet; a chill went over the Assembly so
perceptible that the narrator declared he could not,
at the distance of twenty years, repeat the anecdote
without experiencing again the same sensation.

CHAPTER V.

JOURNEYS IN THE COUNTRY; ATTENDANCE AT COURTS; AMERI-
CAN BISHOPS; LETTERS TO HIS FATHER; EXCURSION INTO
FRANCE; CLERICAL AND LITERARY ASSOCIATES; OPINION OF
CONNECTICUT.

A. D. 1767–1768.

On the 13th of June, Johnson set out in company
with Robert Temple and others on a tour into the
country, visited Oxford where he spent several days,
and then passed on through Stratford-on-Avon, Cov-
entry, Worcester, and Hereford, into Wales, and was·
back again in London by the middle of July, to renew his attention to the Mohegan case, and watch the
interests of the American Colonies. Finding that the
business of his special agency would not require his
continued presence in town, he joined Temple in another excursion, and went to Canterbury on the 17th
of September, where he was very kindly entertained
by Mr. Lance, a brother-in-law of Mr. Temple, whose
" house was situated upon an eminence extremely
pleasant," a mile or two out of the city.

A week was spent in the County of Kent, visiting
various places of historic interest; and having accompanied Temple to Gravesend, where he embarked for
America on the 24th, and taken leave of him, he
returned immediately to London, and entered upon

4

another journey into the North of England. Passing through Norwich, Yarmouth, and East Durham, he arrived on the 5th of October at Weasenham Hall, the country seat of Richard Jackson, in Norfolk, and tarried with him a couple of days. From thence he rode to Tittleshall Church, where he " viewed with a kind of reverence the elegant monument of the great Lord Chief Justice Coke ; " and proceeded to Raynham, " the noble seat of the Lord Viscount Townshend," and viewed the curiosities of that place, and the graves of the family, one of which had been opened just a month before to receive the body of Charles Townshend, the late leader in the House of Commons, whose brilliancy and impetuosity were yet fresh in his remembrance.

This journey was extended through the fen country to Lincoln, Kingston-upon-Hull, and Cherry Burton near Beverley, and was undertaken, among other things, for the purpose of inquiring into the origin of his family, whose ancient seat was at the latter place. He wrote an agreeable letter to his father from York, giving an account of his visit, and of his failure to discover the circumstances attending the emigration of his ancestors.[1]

On returning to London, October 24th, he found one of his American friends (Captain Robinson) sick with the small-pox, to whom he devoted special attention, seeing that all possible care was taken of him, and upon his death he attended his funeral, which was in a church with a sermon, and afterwards solicited from members of his club money to defray the expenses of the illness and burial. Dr. Johnson

[1] See *Life and Correspondence of Samuel Johnson*, pp. 318–320.

at this time was somewhat unwell himself, and sought medical advice; but from the 6th of November, the first day of the term, having paid for a seat in the King's Bench for the term, he was in almost constant attendance in Westminster Hall; hearing a variety of cases tried, and listening to opinions of the Court delivered by Lord Mansfield. He was present in the House of Lords on the 24th of the same month, when, as he noted in his Diary, "the King opened the session of Parliament with a most gracious speech, which he pronounced admirably well."

The consecration of Bishops for America was a subject which lay very near the heart of his venerable father, and he could not refrain from making frequent allusions to it in his letters to his son, and hoped he might have some opportunity of using his influence to good purpose in persuading the rulers of the Church of England to grant the boon. In this, country, "an Appeal to the Public" in behalf of an American Episcopate had been issued, written by Dr. Chandler, of Elizabethtown, N. J., and though sharply attacked, it had been so well defended that reasonable men here could see no objection to the plan proposed. But the untoward course of public events prevented its execution, and led the Home Government to truckle to the spirit of a dominant and intolerant Independency. The "Appeal" was sent to Dr. Johnson in London, by a young man (Mr. Epenetus Townsend) going over for Holy Orders, and in the following letter he acknowledged its reception, and spoke discouragingly of renewing the effort as things then were : —

LONDON, *Jan'y 9th*, 1768.

HONORED SIR, — In my last of the 26th of December to my wife I acknowledged the receipt of yours of the 5th of October by Mr. Townsend and now return you my particular thanks for it, and bless God for the continuance of your health and my own, which remains very good, only I find since my last fall fever I am not quite so robust, and more apt to take colds than I used to be, and am therefore obliged to be more careful of myself, especially since winter set in, which has been quite severe with alternate rain, snow, and frost now near a month.

Mr Townsend seems to be a very worthy man, and I dare say will make a useful clergyman wherever he is placed, but there seems to be some doubt about erecting a new Mission for him at Salem ; yet as he seems to have it much at heart, and I think it would be useful, I shall certainly do him all the service in my power, and have some encouragement from Dr. Burton that it may succeed. I am sorry to hear of Billy Nicholls' death, who I hoped, notwithstanding his wildness, might have at last made a useful man. My time was indeed too short at Oxford, though I made the best I could of every moment of it, and saw almost everything worth notice, but it would give me great pleasure to review the principal of them again with more leisure and attention, but I am not sure I shall be able to effect it.

The Appeal (which was delivered me by Mr. Townsend) is an excellent performance, and will at least, I hope, tend to soften the minds of those in America who have been averse to this design, as well as stimulate those who have been lukewarm and prepare them against some more fortunate juncture, which may some time or other perhaps happen here ; but at present it will I believe have no effect in this country, nor be at all attended to by any of those who can alone effectuate a matter of this nature. You do not know enough (give me leave to say) of the true state of this country, nor its present policy so far as it has any, to judge properly of this affair, nor can I explain it fully, till I see you. If I find it has any effect, I will let you know — meantime continue to practice that Christian patience you have so long exercised, and satisfied that you have now done all you can, make yourselves as easy about it as you can.

I have been very unlucky in not meeting Mr. Parkhurst, having been twice at his house in Epsom and he as often at my lodgings without success. But our friend Mr. Berkeley I have had several conversations with. He is a most friendly, communicative, pious man, perhaps a little too severe and warm upon some occasions. He has a worse opinion of the moral and political state of things here, if possible, than I have, and makes most grievous complaints of the decay of piety and orthodoxy and the increase of Deism, Socinianism, and Irreligion. The Hutchinsonians, he says, have been imprudent, and laid too much stress upon trifles in many instances; but the general System is by no means decaying, but rather gaining ground, and he thinks must and will flourish. He laments much the situation of Mr Jones, who is declining in health and he thinks cannot live long. He affirms that he is without exception the most learned man now in the three kingdoms. When he wrote upon the Trinity and Natural Philosophy, he had only a poor curacy of about £25 per annum, and was, with his family, chiefly supported by the charity of the Hutchinsonians at Oxford, but has now a living of £300 per annum in Kent, given him by the good Abp., and being thus at ease had it in intention to have wrote many things would his health have permitted. Horne, he says, is steadfast and will never fail; he thinks him one of the best of men, meek, though zealous, a sincere Christian as well as a most learned man. He likes Parkhurst's Lexicon, and thinks the Greek one of the New Testament, which he is publishing, will be also a very good performance. He has a warm affection for you and for the memory of my dear brother, and bid me tell you that he envies your happiness in America, where he thinks there is much orthodoxy and true piety — bids you in God's name not to be discouraged, but all go on to establish the foundations laid there; and whether the lukewarm people here will take any notice of you or not, since the cause is of God, it must and will flourish and the gates of Hell cannot prevail against it. A departure from the true Faith and the neglect of vital piety has, says he, in a manner undone us here, and if we do not reform will soon complete our ruin; and the adherence to the one and practice of the other will as surely build you up in America, and render that country the asylum of all good men, even from hence, who will ·ere long be obliged to fly there from the boundless impiety and approaching destruction of this dissolute and abandoned nation.

This is a specimen of Mr Berkeley's general conversation, his particular anecdotes of kings and persons are too many, and most of them too pointed to put into writing, but will serve very well for the amusement of conversation. He is not alone, I find, in his idea of America's becoming a refuge at the ruin of this country; many of the friends of the Colonies think they see the period hastening, and rejoice that they have open to them so happy a retreat and are for that reason I believe the more our friends. I have a letter from Mr B. since Christmas, in which he desires me to present you his Mother's, his Lady's, and his own compliments of that holy season, and promises to be in town again sometime in February. My last contained a full account of the late change of Administration (or rather, intended one, for it is not yet completed, though absolutely depended upon), since which nothing material has occurred: Neither the Abp. of York nor the Bp. of Oxford are yet come to town. Mention to me some other pictures, for I find none of those you desired can be procured, unless it be the Abp. of York's, and that only as a favor, which, however, I cannot yet obtain, though I expect I shall. Don't by any means send me your Bills, if you have any occasion for them. Dear Billy's good promises give me much satisfaction, and if he performs them I shall think nothing too much for him. I have only to add my sincerest duty to you and tenderest love to my wife and children, with compliments to all friends, and remain

Honored Sir, your most dutiful son and humble servant,

WM. SAML. JOHNSON.

Scarcely a month had elapsed when he wrote again to his father, to allay any anxiety which he might have about his health, and to inform him that the slow progress of the Mohegan business would prevent his immediate return. It sounds strangely in our ears to hear a political election seriously offered as a reason for inattention to a matter which concerned only the order and government of the Church of England in America. But it shows how difficult it was, in the peculiar state of the times, for Bishops and Statesmen to separate, in their views of public duty, spiritual from temporal things. The letter was dated, —

LONDON, *February 6th,* 1768.

HONORED SIR, — I thank you for your kind congratulations on my recovery from my late illness, and hope there is no great danger of my relapsing into those disorders, as you seem to apprehend. The opening the Churchyard might perhaps have some share in my illness; my friend Jackson thinks as you do that it had, but I rather fancy not. You may depend upon it, I shall take all due care of myself, and if I should be ill again will have proper help. Your friend Dr. Nicholls I doubt not is equal to any of the profession, but he has left off business and retired to Oxford. The physician I had is very eminent and the best I ever saw, at least in one respect, as he prescribes as few medicines as possible and none but with great caution. But I hope I shall have no further occasion for any of them, as at present, I thank God, I am very well, and under His protection have great reason to hope for the continuance of my health, as the weather is now growing every day more and more favorable and spring will soon open upon us.

Mason was indeed dilatory enough, but he some time ago put his business into another person's hands, who seems very desirous of bringing it on, so that the cause will not now be delayed for want of pushing; and as I mentioned in my last (of the 28th of Jany. to my wife) there is now a good prospect of its coming on ere long. But let me still beg that you will make yourselves easy about me. I will do all in my power to hasten my return, and in God's good time hope for a happy meeting with you. I am much concerned at the trouble you have about getting an Assistant, but hope you will make yourself easy in the affair, since having fully done your part towards it, it now remains with the people to second your endeavors, or bear with patience the inconveniences which may happen for want of one. I am glad the Pamphlets are agreeable, but I do not wish it should be known here, while I continue in England, that I sent them to America. A large parcel was certainly sent to N. York.

A few days ago I waited upon the Abps. of Canterbury and York; the first is ill with the gout, and I could not say very much to him. As to reprinting the piece you mention, he thought it might be well to be first considered by the Society, or at least by the Bps. at some of their meetings, and as soon as his health would permit he would have it taken into consideration. The Abp. of York received me very kindly; he is a lively, facetious, sensible, and active man, and went very fully into the subject of your letter (for which he thanks you); and after having gone through all the steps he had taken in the affair for several years past, in which it seems he has been very assiduous, and recounted the difficulties attending it, he finally fixed upon this — that supposing it possible to get over every other objection, yet the present time was by no means proper to attempt anything of this nature, as it would be utterly impossible to gain any attention to it, while the Ministers, and indeed every body else, were so intent upon the business of the approaching Election, so that some more favorable juncture must be waited for, but when that would arrive he could not foresee.

The Bp. of Oxford, whom I waited upon next, was of the same opinion as to this matter. I presented him your Grammar, for which, as well as your letter, he returns you many thanks, and said he was highly honored by it. Parkhurst he had never seen, but would at your request examine it and be able to give some opinion of it. The author of the Notes on his Prelections (about which you desired me to inquire) he says is a learned, sensible man, of great freedom of sentiment and extent of thought, much superior to the generality of the German Divines. He does not, he says, agree to all he has said in his Notes, but upon the whole they are sensible and ingenious. You will see when Michaelis wrote his first Part, he thought Lowth was dead, though he was afterwards better informed, and they have since had a literary correspondence between them. The Bp. is very glad that the study of Hebrew is like to have some footing in America, and pleased with your endeavors to promote it, and will I fancy write to you upon the subject. Faden tells me Pike's Lexicon is simply an abridgment of Parkhurst, and (though he printed it) of no use to those who have the original. He proposes to send the Lexicons and Grammars as you advise to Parker of N York, by the ships now about to sail. The 2d Part of the Introduction, etc., is now ready for the Press, but it will, he says, be several months before he can print it. He says he will allow you for the Copy, 50 Grammars (besides those already sent you, and half a dozen I have to give away), 25 of which shall be bound and the rest stitched. Those I have I will present as you direct. If you think he does not allow you enough for the Copy tell me and I will insist on more.

The Act permitting the importation of salt beef, pork, butter, and hams from America is now passed, beside which nothing material to the Colonies has happened since I last wrote. I got an acquaintance of mine, who is intimate with Lord Lyttleton, to mention you to him as having a value for his writings and wishing to see his picture, and to know of him whether he had any Plate, etc. His Lordship in answer desired his compliments to you, and thanks for taking so much notice of him, but said no picture had ever been taken of him, though his bookseller had requested one to prefix to his Life of Henry II., and perhaps he should consent to it when he had finished that work. Mr. Townsend's affair is settled with great dispatch, agreeable to his wish, and, to use Dr. Burton's expression, pursuant to your recommendation, to which they pay the greatest regard. He is now returning, and by him I shall send Foster's Hebrew Bible, Michaelis' Notes (which by the way are never bound up with the Prelections, of which there has been no other edition but that you have), and as many Grammars as Faden can get ready.

I am with the tenderest love to my dear wife and children and compliments to all friends,

Honored Sir,

Your most dutiful son and humble servant,

WM. SAMUEL JOHNSON.

His prolonged stay in England, though unexpected by himself and wearisome to his family, gave him an opportunity of traveling in different sections of the country, and of making brief visits on the Continent. From the 15th of March, 1768, to the first week in April, he was on a journey into France, and upon his return to England, heard nothing for some time so earnestly discussed among his friends as the result of the London and Middlesex elections — the latter of which was in favor of John Wilkes, who had been expelled from the House of Commons, four years before, for a libelous attack upon the King, and who was now returned amid much popular tumult in spite of the stigma upon his character.

But the chief business of Dr. Johnson, aside from his special agency, and from other public and private affairs intrusted to him, was to watch the measures of Parliament, and by conference with leading minds in Church and State to endeavor to discover the temper of Englishmen towards Americans. Governor Trumbull was not sorry for his detention in such critical times, and his letters to him and to his friends are a graphic picture of the progress of events charged as they were with momentous consequences. Saintly Secker, then Archbishop of Canterbury, the life-long correspondent of his venerated father, and the defender of the Church of England in America, the elegant and scholarly Lowth, Newton, the Bishop of Bristol, and Terrick, the Bishop of London, these among prelates; the younger Berkeley, Burton, Horne, the Commentator on the Psalms, Jones of Nayland, Parkhurst, Porteus, Stinton, among the clergy; Barre, Burke, Chatham, Conway, Dunning, Mansfield, Pringle, Wedderburn, among political characters; all were his warm friends, and many of them helped him, as they had the opportunity and power, in the business of his agency. The great English Lexicographer, Dr. Samuel Johnson, who had not yet learned to hate Americans with intense hatred, became particularly fond of his transatlantic namesake, and claimed relationship with him, though it is not probable the connection was very carefully traced or very clearly established.

The more intimately he associated with Englishmen, the kinder he found them in their disposition towards Americans. Nothing surprised him so much as their deplorable lack of general information concerning the Colonists and the geography of the country. Oftentimes he must have smiled at the measure of ignorance blended with credulity, and once it is believed he could not have refrained from laughing outright when he heard the character of Connecticut given in a letter from a sojourner in this country to his friend in London. The letter was written in 1768, and the portion which described the character was copied by Johnson, and is too good to be lost even though it should not make

> " Our ancestry a gallant, Christian race,
> Patterns of every virtue, every grace. "

This London friend seems to have directed inquiries with a view to an investment in the Colony either for speculation or occupancy, and the answer returned was : " Without mentioning names, I have consulted Mr. —— about the American affair, who says it will not do : he says he would not give £800 for the whole Province ; that he has been all over it at New Haven and New London ; that they are all mortgaged to the full to the Bostonians and New Yorkers ; that they have all their goods from those two places, and import very little ; very few merchants, chiefly farmers, all upon a level, labor very dear, spirit Oliverians, but very great rogues, no money amongst them, and nobody would live amongst them that could possibly live anywhere else ! "

CHAPTER VI.

A. D. 1768–1769.

THE popular tumults, the violence, and the mobs
occasioned by the election of Wilkes to Parliament extended into various parts of the kingdom, and one
town in Lancashire was fairly desolated and pillaged,
not a house being left with windows or doors un-
broken. After his election, he appeared on the first
day of term in the King's Bench, and in a "set
speech" surrendered himself to the judgment and
laws of his country, but at the same time accused the
Chief Justice (Lord Mansfield) of having illegally and
injuriously altered to his prejudice the record upon
which he was tried. Subsequently he applied for a
writ of error for the reversal of the sentence of out-
lawry against him, which was learnedly argued, and
"every time," says Johnson, "the matter was moved
in court, Westminster Hall and all the avenues to it
were crowded with an amazing concourse of people."
Indeed, he added, writing to his father May 14, "we
seem here to be almost in a state of anarchy, there
being beside this of Wilkes's five other mobs assembled,

viz., the sailors (who in a body of six or eight thousand went down on Wednesday and delivered a petition to Parliament, but behaved with much decency), the coal-heavers, sawyers, journeymen hatters, and weavers, all complaining of the excessive price of provisions, and insisting upon an advancement of their wages. By this rising of the seamen, the maritime trade of London has been several days totally stopped, and no ship can go down the river. These several mobs are yet independent of each other, but a general discontent is visible among the people, and if government cannot discover some method to quiet them before they unite, the most fatal consequences may be apprehended."

It was thus a good opportunity to stir up strife, and for a man of the "most abandoned principles and dissolute manners in private life," who had insulted his sovereign, and as Pitt said, "blasphemed his God," to become for the time being a popular favorite. The judgments against Wilkes were finally. twenty-two months imprisonment, £1000 fine, and surety for good behavior for seven years, which his friends at first thought very severe, but with calmer passions came quiet acquiescence. This disturbed state of affairs at home absorbed the attention of government, and little consideration was given during its continuance to the interests of the American Colonies.

Taking advantage of every convenient opportunity to improve the civilities offered to his acceptance, Johnson rode out to Acton and spent Sunday, the 19th of June, with his good friend Dr. Berkeley. He heard him preach in the morning and his curate in the afternoon, and after noting in his Diary the events of the day, he added : " The church at Acton was built by Oliver Cromwell, and many of his friends resided there, as Skippon, whose wife had a monument in the church. Mr. Baxter also lived there, and the great and good Chief Justice Hale, whose house I saw, — a large ancient structure. Old Mrs. Berkeley," the late Bishop of Cloyne's lady, — of whom he spoke as very affectionate and kind, and retaining great fondness for America, — " was a Foster, descended from Monck, Earl of Albemarle, and the Doctor has called his eldest son, for that reason, George Monck." His intimacy with this family was one of the bright spots of his sojourn in England, and brought him in contact with many persons of worth and distinction.

The Archbishop of Canterbury died suddenly on the 3d of August, 1768, and the Church in both hemispheres was deprived of a wise and careful counselor. He was one of the best of men, and had long taken a deep interest in the religious welfare of the Colonies. In a letter to his father announcing the tidings of his death, Johnson said : " God can and certainly will take care of His own cause and interest in the world, but in truth I see no prospect that anybody here will make good the Archbishop's ground. Several of the Bishops are very worthy men, but none of them in my opinion by any means so well qualified for that high station as the late Archbishop."

The vision of the future was thus to him gloomy, and he had many fears that less attention and aid than formerly would be given to religion in America. " The Church of England there," said he, in the same letter to his father, " should in fact think more of taking care of itself. The Society will indeed, I trust, still continue to afford their friendly assistance, but even that is a precarious dependence, and I wish my countrymen not to rely too much upon it, but prepare themselves as far as possible to stand upon their own ground. The affection between that country and this seems to be every day decreasing, and the growing jealousies on both sides threaten the destruction of all our harmony and happiness ; already there is hardly any other cement left between us beside the interest founded in trade, and even that is declining. Let us look forward and see where these things must end, and consider what must probably be soon the state of that country and this. I was going to imagine it with respect to religion. But in truth I dare not pursue these reflections farther upon paper."

The new Archbishop, Dr. Cornwallis, though a good and noble prelate, did not command the high respect of his predecessor, or wield the same influence in directing the operations of the Society for the Propagation of the Gospel in Foreign Parts.

What Johnson feared for the Church, he had begun to fear far more for his country. He could not be blind to the scenes that were enacted around him, and so early as April, 1769, he wrote to Dr. Benjamin Gale, of Killingworth, Connecticut, and foreshadowed a separation from England. "With regard to American affairs," said he in this letter, " we are told nothing farther is proposed to be done in this session of Parliament unless something should occur in America to render it necessary. The petitions and applications for a repeal of the laws are all rejected or laid aside, and we are told they must first see that we are disposed to submit to Parliamentary regulations, and have given some proofs of our humility and good disposition towards them before it can be done. Those proofs of submission I do not expect America will give them, and, therefore, they will not I fancy have again so good an opportunity to repeal those acts as they have at present; and it seems pretty probable that we shall go on contending and fretting each other till your prophecy shall, as it certainly will be, fulfilled, and we become separate and independent empires. That this event is hastening with rapid progress, and that it will be certainly fatal to Great Britain, is so very apparent that one wonders that they do not both see and wisely labor to prevent it. Whether we should wish it or endeavor to prevent it depends on the course we might take after such separation should take place. If we were wise and could form some system of free government upon just principles, we might be very happy without any connection with this country. But should we ever agree upon anything of this nature? Should we not more probably fall into factions and parties amongst ourselves, destroy one another, and become at length an easy prey of the first invader? This at least is to be feared, and should teach us as well as Britain to manage the present dispute between us with some degree of moderation and temper."

In the lull of political commotions, and while his presence in London was not needed to promote the Mohegan case, he made a visit to Canterbury, and the following letter to his father, though containing severe animadversions upon a portion of the clergy of the Church of England at that period, is too full of

5

interest and pleasant description to be omitted from these pages : —

CANTERBURY, *Sept.* 12*th*, 1769.

HONORED SIR, — When I wrote you the 18th of August I acquainted you I should soon see Dr. Berkeley; accordingly I made him a visit at Cookham, and as he was about setting out to perform his prebendarial residence here, he would admit of no excuse from my accompanying him to this city, where I have now been this fortnight leading the life of an ecclesiastic, at church twice a day, and seeing nobody but Deans, Archdeacons, Prebendaries, and Priests; very good company you will say and a good employment. They are so, and it is certainly a sober, quiet, good kind of an idle life. The Dean, a son of the late Abp. Potter, is a good, sensible, polite, friendly man, but a good deal out of health, and is now gone to drink the waters of Tunbridge. The Archdeacon and Vice Dean, Sir John Head, is one of the most amiable men I have met with in England, was a particular friend of the late Archbishop, and very highly esteemed by him. As he is a baronet of family and fortune, besides his preferments in the Church, he lives in much elegance and magnificence, but preserves the character of a serious, faithful divine, as well as of a good man and a polite gentleman. Dr. Walwin, the eldest Prebendary, is also an excellent man, and very learned, but is severely afflicted with an asthma which it is feared will prove fatal to him. Dr. Dampier, Dr. Durell (late Vice Chancellor of the University of Oxford), Mr. Benson, etc., whom I have seen, seem also to be very worthy men ; but there are two or three others whom I have not seen nor wish to see, who have been lately preferred through the interest of Lord Granby, whose characters are very indifferent, and who, like, alas! too many of the superior clergy of England, have little virtue and less religion, who obtain their preferments without merit, merely by Court favor, or family connections, and are a reproach to their profession, which they consider solely as a means of procuring wealth to be avariciously hoarded for a provision for a family, or vilely squandered in vice and dissipation, or, at best, consumed in luxury, indolence, and ease, while they care no more about religion or the Church, or anything else that is virtuous or praiseworthy, than they do for the miracles or mosques of Mahomet, and I fear, believe just as much of the one as of the other. Alas, how is the gold become dim, and the most fine gold changed! Upon this sad subject I could *a Tale unfold, which* (in the expressive phrase of Shakespeare) *would harrow up your soul*, but I cannot bear to give you pain, and decline a subject which makes my own heart ache whenever it occurs. Yet in my own justification, I must just touch one character. You say you wish to know why I have so indifferent an opinion of his lordship of ———, and ask why I do not apply more to him. Time is lost in paying court to such men. He is in those things wherein you hope he may be useful a perfect Gallio; he cares for none of them. He is more of a politician and courtier, I fear, than a Christian or a divine; and yet even his politics are confined to a very narrow sphere. He is, perhaps, the greatest card-player in England. He does not indeed, as far as I know, play deep, as the phrase is, but six hours in six days in a week hardly suffice for this favorite amusement. He is — but I forbear — *ex pede Herculem* — Peace to all such. Yet thank God there are some burning and shining lights yet left in this dark age, by whom the sacred fire will still, I trust, be kept alive, and from whom it may catch and spread into a flame, whenever it shall please God that His Church shall be again bright as the sun in its glory, and terrible as an army with banners, not indeed in the pomp and splendor of worldly power and prerogative, — to which some I fear are apt to apply such expressions, — but spiritually glorious; splendid by the purity of her faith and institutions; bright by the piety, zeal, and ability of her ministers; glorious by her influence upon the hearts and lives of all her members, and terrible to all the powers of darkness by pushing her conquests into their remotest territories, and confounding their empire by converting their subjects, and changing the children of Satan and slaves of darkness into the sons of God, and heirs of light and immortality. But I forget whom I am writing to, and return to tell you that I have spent a good deal of time here with your old friend Mr. Gosling, one of the Minor Canons, who, though he has been long confined to his chamber, and will be able to go abroad no more, having lost the use of his legs by the gout, is still very hearty, cheerful, and gay. He remembers you with much affection, and my brother with regard for his memory. Here, too (that I may remind you of a scene which must have given you pleasure), I have been more than once into the tower of the Cathedral, where I see your and your friends' names inscribed when you were here, and from whence there is an extensive prospect of one of the finest, richest, and best cultivated counties in England. The Cathedral is kept in excellent repair by the Dean and Chapter, and I need not tell you is a most noble structure, though not equal to those of York and Lincoln, which are also preserved in good condition, though not so well as this, — a circumstance much to the honor of this Chapter, especially when compared with several others in the kingdom, who have rapaciously appropriated to themselves the revenues which should have repaired their churches, by which alone, as Abp. Secker used to say, they live, and which, having been shamefully neglected, are hanging in ruins over the heads of those who are sacrilegiously rioting in their spoils. The repairs of this church I find are commonly annually about £1200 ; and yet the Deanery is worth £1000, and the Prebends from £300 to £400 per annum, beside their livings, which they take in succession as they fall, which are from £100 to £200 per annum a piece ; so that the whole annual revenue of this corporation, including the school belonging to it, may be fairly estimated at about £10,000 per annum. A noble foundation !

I propose to leave Canterbury very soon, and shall spend a day or two with Sir George Oxenden, whose seat is in this neighborhood, with whom I have before made an acquaintance. He is a joyous old knight, who was one of the Lords of the Admiralty during great part of Sir Robert Walpole's administration, and one of his bosom friends ; he is consequently a master of all the politics of that period, nor has he been inattentive to what has passed since. He takes pleasure in comparing those times with the present, from whence one may derive both amusement and instruction. He took care (as most of them do) to secure a fortune while he was in power ; and now lives in all the splendor of a prince without caring who are out or in. From thence I shall return to London, where I hope to hear soon of the continuance of your health, and that of my dear family, whom God preserve.

I am afraid I omitted to acquaint you, as I intended in my last, that Faden thinks he cannot yet publish a second edition of the Grammar, though he says he hopes he may by and by venture upon it. By some negligence or other it was not published in a long time after it was printed, and you know books of this kind can sell but slowly, as at most the purchasers can be but few. A thousand volumes of politics, novels, or nonsense may be sold to a single one that has a word of Hebrew in it, which instantly frightens three quarters of mankind, and is thought by much the greater part of the other quarter not worth their attention.

Did I ever tell you that I judged right about the Bishop of Oxford, in relation to degrees ? His situation, he intimated, gave him no authority, nor his connections any interest, which could be employed that way. Indeed, he said, it was even improper for any churchman, other than the Abp. of Canterbury for the time being, to ask favors of that kind, and how far the present Archbishop would be inclined to solicit, he did not know, but thought he would not be backward upon proper occasions. I find the Archbishop is making Lambeth Doctors, so that perhaps he would choose that application should be made *to*, rather than *through* him, as the first is attended with some emolument, and there can be none in the latter method. I am, perhaps, almost as delicate as the Bishop of Oxford upon this subject, and should not much like to ask the present Archbishop for his interest at Oxford ; but if you think proper to write him such a request, in favor of any friends you would oblige, in your own name, I will venture to deliver the letter and back it, and at least bring you off decently with him, if it does not succeed. But take care who you recommend, for the Oxonians are very nice upon this subject. They refused a degree, you know, to the Bishop of Gloucester, and have repented of many they have given, though I flatter myself of none they have honored us with in America. Those whose degrees cost them £120 sterling, as is commonly the case with those who are created Doctors in the common course, are very jealous, when others obtain the like honors without either expense or labor, and they are to the last degree solicitous that their diplomas especially should not be prostituted as those of the Scotch Universities have been. You know, I doubt not, that these degrees are not merely honorary like those conferred at the public Encœnia, or when great persons visit the University, but entitle, in the language of the diploma, *ad Omnia Jura et Privilegia*, give a right to sit and vote, upon all occasions, in Convocation, and for members of Parliament, as well as many other important privileges, so that they have some reason, beside the reputation of it, to be careful who they confer them upon.

There is no very material news, and I will not trouble you with a word of politics, about which, though a very fruitful subject, everything must be very uncertain till the meeting of Parliament, but with my tenderest love to my dearest wife and children, and compliments to all friends, remain

Honored Sir, your most dutiful son and humble servant,

WM. SAML. JOHNSON.

His return to London was followed by the resumption of his usual duties, and indulgence in his usual entertainments. On Wednesday, the 18th of October, he speaks in his Diary of having " made a visit to Dr. Johnson at Whiston's," and the next day he visited him again, and spent all the morning conversing chiefly upon literary subjects, and hearing from him " several anecdotes of the late Mr. Richardson, Mallet, Milton, Bishop Lowth, Warburton, King Charles I.," and others. A letter to his father, written about this time, gives a brief account of his first interview with the great man who fills so high a place in English literature, as well as a sketch of his recent tour on the Continent, which for special reasons he had not before communicated : —

WESTMINSTER, *Nov.* 2, 1769.

. . . . For the sake of the name, and because I think him one of the best of the modern writers, I made an acquaintance, some time ago, with Dr. Samuel Johnson, author of the Dictionary, etc. He was very well pleased with the attention I paid him, had heard of you, and presents his compliments. He has shining abilities, great erudition, exact and extensive knowledge, is ranked in the first class of the literati, and highly esteemed for his strong sense and virtue ; but is as odd a mortal, in point of behavior and appearance, as you ever saw. You would not, at first sight, suspect he had ever read, or thought, in his life, or was much above the degree of an idiot. But *nulla fronti fides*, when he opens himself, after a little acquaintance, you are abundantly repaid for these first unfavorable appearances.

It is hardly worth while to say anything to you relating to political affairs. Everything of this kind must be particularly uncertain till Parliament meets, and that, it is believed, is not intended to sit for dispatch of business till after Christmas. In the mean time many counties, cities, and boroughs are zealously petitioning his Majesty for the dissolution of the House of Commons, and many people begin to think it will take place ; but as it would be a very fatal stroke to the present Ministry, who have great influence with the King, I do not, for my own part, yet think it will be done. The struggles of party continue as violent as ever, and the uneasiness and discontents amongst the people are equally great and general, but how they will end can be but illy guessed at present. There has been much talk of late that the Lord Chancellor (who is, upon the whole, the best man amongst them) would soon be dismissed from administration, and it is certain there has been some altercation between him and the other ministers, upon the affair of the Middlesex election; but it rather seems now as if it would blow over. We imagine we are very near the crisis of some considerable political revolutions, but it may nevertheless be some time, perhaps, before anything very decisive takes place.

For reasons formerly hinted at, I did not intend you should have known, till my return, any more of my excursion this summer than of that of the last, but I find I can conceal nothing from you. Captain Scott was, however, a little mistaken. I was not going to France, with which I was satisfied in my former jaunt. It was the tour of Holland, Brabant, and Flanders that I made. I passed from Harwich to Helvoetsluys, visited all the principal towns, both of North and South Holland; then went from Rotterdam, by water, to Dort, Williamstadt, and Bergen op Zoom, up the Scheldt to Antwerp, made an excursion to Breda, to see the Prince of Orange, who lay encamped in that neighborhood with 8 or 10,000 men, learning the art of war; then went by Mechlin, etc., to Brussels, returned by the way of Ghent, Bruges, and Ostend, landed at Dover, and arrived again in London, all in about six weeks. A most agreeable ramble! And had I known then as I do now that I could not have finished my business, and returned this fall to America, I certainly should have gone on, and made the tour of Italy, which I might very well have done, in very agreeable company, and been in England again by this time, without any prejudice to my affairs. As it has turned out, it is, I own, with some regret that I have lost so good an opportunity of treading upon classic ground, and visiting a country which has been the scene of so many interesting transactions, and is the repository of the most curious monuments of antiquity. But the less is said upon this subject in Connecticut, perhaps, the better.

Do not, however, imagine that by indulging my curiosity, and being conversant with the grandeur and delicacies of Europe, I shall be tempted to disregard or look down upon America, or that home will appear mean or despicable to me. My attachments there are too strong ever to be relaxed. The true felicities of life, after all, are, in my opinion, of the domestic kind, and to be found in moderate situations. Better is the dinner of herbs, and the humble cottage, with one's friends and tender connections about one, than all the splendor and delicacies of the gay or great world, without them. I will not have the vanity to impute it to my philosophy, but it is my good fortune, that though I am pleased enough with seeing these things yet they take little hold of my affections. I like to look behind the gay curtain, but when I do I find little to admire and less to be attached to. I see it very generally true, that the more people *possess* the less they *enjoy*. Riches, state, magnificence, etc., cast a deceitful glare around all objects, both persons and things, which at a distance wonderfully magnifies them, and makes one imagine them to be very desirable ; as we approach nearer, the deception vanishes, and we too often find them mean, contemptible, and exceedingly deficient in all intrinsic worth. Yet many good uses may be made of these approaches to high life ; and as not the least of them I flatter myself that you will find me less attached to the grandeur of the world by all I have seen of it, and that I shall be the more contented in a humble situation for having passed so much time in higher scenes. My *wishes*, were they indulged me to the utmost, would be very limited, and all center in a little ease and independence in the tranquil vales of America. The worst of it is, that I am not like to be very soon gratified even in such humble hopes, and the best way is (to which I hope to bring myself by and by) to have no *wishes* for anything in this world but what we actually possess, or have certainly within our reach. This however cannot be till I return to Stratford. My uppermost *wish*, at present, is to see you and my dear family, to whom I present my tenderest love, and remain in perfect health (blessed be God), with compliments to all friends,

Honored Sir, your most dutiful son and humble servant,

WM. SAML. JOHNSON.

CHAPTER VII.

TAXATION OF THE COLONIES; SCHEME OF AMERICAN BISHOPS;
LETTER TO HIS FATHER; SEVERE ILLNESS; LETTER TO HIS
SON-IN-LAW; ANXIETY ABOUT HIS FAMILY; FINAL HEARING
OF THE MOHEGAN CAUSE; RETURN TO AMERICA, AND THANKS
OF THE GENERAL ASSEMBLY.

A. D. 1769–1771.

Notwithstanding the disposition in England to
lay burdens upon the Colonies and reduce them to
subjection, Johnson was inclined to think that it was
best for them to be submissive, for a time at least,
rather than refractory. He knew the weakness and
poverty of his own country, and his personal observations for a period of nearly five years made him
acquainted with the strength and resources of Great
Britain. In the beginning of 1769 he wrote to his
father and spoke of what seemed to be the fixed resolution of the Administration not to repeal immediately those acts which the Colonies complained of,
but to maintain the right of Parliament to impose
duties and taxes in America, and to enforce obedience
to its laws in the most effectual manner. Four months
later, writing again with scarcely pleasanter forebod-
ings, he said: "It is extremely unhappy that we
cannot on both sides come to a better temper in the
unfortunate dispute now subsisting between this coun-

try and that. If we once get into blood, your conjecture will undoubtedly be too soon fatally verified; we shall destroy each other, and become an easy prey to our enemies. Prudent men, on both sides, are aware of this danger, and will, I hope, by degrees gain so much influence as to prevent it. Administration have, since the rising of Parliament, given out that the duty act shall be repealed next year, if the Colonies' remain quiet, but one can hardly depend much upon the declarations of ministers."

The year rolled away and no material change appeared in the policy of the British Government. Johnson wrote to Governor Trumbull of Connecticut, on the 16th of October, 1769, and stated how the hope was entertained that " the disagreements of the Southern from the Northern Colonies" might effect the subjection of all to the legislative power of Great Britain. " In truth," he added, " though my knowing neighbor says otherwise, I begin to think Parliament will be dissolved. If the Americans unite at this most critical juncture, they may carry their point. If they do not now unite, effectual care will be taken to prevent their uniting to any purpose at any future period."

The scheme of sending Bishops to America was one which disturbed the minds of many people in this country; and when Governor Trumbull inquired what were the intentions in England relative to it, he was answered by the Colony's agent that " it is not intended at present to send any Bishops into the American Colonies. Had it been, I should certainly have acquainted you with it; and should it be done at all, you may be assured it will be in such manner as in no degree to prejudice, or if possible even give the least offence to any denomination of Protestants. It has indeed been merely a religious, in no respect a political scheme. As I am myself of the Church of England, you will not doubt that I have had the fullest opportunity to be intimately acquainted with all the steps that have been ever taken in this affair, and you may rely upon it, that it never was nor is the intention, or even wish of those who have been most sanguine in the matter, that American Bishops should have any the least degree of secular power of any nature or kind whatsoever, much less any manner of concern or connection with Christians of any other denomination."

The state of political affairs was still tumultuous enough in England, and he knew very well that while it lasted no attention would be given to a scheme which had been so much debated and misunderstood as that of sending Bishops to the American Colonies. "When these things will end no man can tell," were words which he wrote to his father on the 28th of March, 1770, after he had been speaking of the disorders growing out of the remonstrance of the Livery of London, the King's answer, the address of Parliament thereon, and the remonstrance of Westminster and of the Middlesex freeholders. "We are not to expect, I believe, more for America than the repeal of the duties upon paper, glass, and painters' colors in this session of Parliament, nor consequently can the trade be opened."

The business of his special agency "dragged its slow length along," and he grew more and more impatient under the delays to which he was subjected.

His family, now increased by the marriage of his eldest daughter to the **Rev. Ebenezer Kneeland,** importuned him to return, and it filled them with disappointment and added to his own solicitude for their welfare when his expectations to do so failed year after year to be realized. The following letter to his father shows the depth of his anxieties on the subject, and mentions a severe illness which had left him in no condition to embark for America, even if his business had then been completed : —

WESTMINSTER, *Aug.* 18*th*, 1770.

HONORED AND DEAR SIR, — I have omitted writing to you for some time past in firm confidence that I should very soon have embraced you, but it has pleased God, to my very great grief and affliction, to order otherwise, and I must now renew my correspondence with the disagreeable intelligence that I have not only been unable to get my business dispatched, but have, for this month past, been extremely ill with a severe fit of the gout in both my feet, which, though blessed be God, it has gone off well, has left me so lame, weak, and low, that I am, at present, in no condition to embark for America if my business were finished, or had I determined to abandon it, as I have been strongly inclined to do. Never was I so much at a loss what to do in my life. Were there any room to imagine this Mohegan cause might not be tried in five or six months, I should not hesitate to come away as soon as my health would permit, though to return again, should it be thought necessary, to attend the trial, which I had almost concluded to do before I was taken sick ; but there is now no hope of its being postponed so long ; it must be finished in the autumn, as soon as the Lords of Council come to town, or at farthest in the Christmas Holidays. Having entered upon it, and gone so far, they cannot help finishing it one way or another. Then, on the one hand, to leave the cause under these circumstances, and just at the crisis of it, after so long an attendance, seems to be attended with many difficulties. It looks as if I should incur the resentment of all that are in any measure interested in the affair, — that is of the whole Colony, — and the ridicule of all mankind, which, besides the dishonor of it, would ruin me in my business, and bring destruction on my family.

On the other hand, to think of continuing here longer in the present situation of my family, my private affairs, and especially of my wife, distresses me to the last degree. Thus beset with troubles, I have, to use General Wolfe's expression, only a choice of difficulties, and on which side to determine, I own I am at a loss. How happy should I be could you advise me. My friends here, indeed, unanimously agree that I ought to see the end of my business, at least to stay three or four months longer ; but then they know not half the distress of my family, nor mine on their account. The consideration what in the mean time will become of my poor dear wife and family, with me absorbs almost every other consideration. At present my duty to my family as well as myself seems to direct that I should attend first, as far as I can, to the recovery of my health, which, to tell you the truth, has never been quite such as it used to be since that terrible fever I had here three years ago ; but my physicians tell me may now, after so regular a fit of the gout, be very firm for several years, if I am but careful in my recovery, for which purpose I suppose they will advise me, as soon as I can, to get out into the country. But what I shall do next, whether embark for America, or see the end of my cause, in truth I cannot now determine, and can only pray God to direct me for the best.

Much cause have I to complain of the gout. The Attorney General's gout alone prevented our cause being finished in June, and I should then probably have been at this time, where I so anxiously wish to be, at Stratford ; mine has baffled all my schemes to prevent or overcome the ill consequences of his illness. One mitigating circumstance, however, attends it, that one can bear with more patience those

ills which are the immediate infliction of Providence, than
those which are occasioned by the faults of men.   Had this
delay been occasioned by anything less than sickness or
unavoidable necessity, I should have had no patience left.
But nobody is to blame ; it was the act of Providence.   Indeed, one may justly think it hard that the Lords, in so
extraordinary a case as this, would not delay their going
down to their country seats till Mr. De Grey's recovery, or
even return again to town to try it at any time ; but this is
so unusual, and it is so fixed a rule to do no business at this
season of the year, that it would hardly be expected of them,
and the long established custom affords them some excuse.
Every way, however, it is a sad misfortune to me, and the
disappointment to you and my family gives me inexpressible
concern.   I know you will give all the consolation you can
to my poor dear wife, to whom I have suggested all the foregoing considerations, and whatever else occurred, but alas !
how much after all do I fear for her.

I am infinitely obliged to you for your several letters which
have come to hand down to the 31st of May, without which
I should have known nothing of your situation, which would
have redoubled my anxiety.   The continuance of your and
the family's health fills me with the sincerest gratitude to
God.   I hope you will have written again by the Packet,
which is hourly expected, and that I shall have the great
satisfaction to find you continue in health, — the only satisfaction I can have in my present situation.

The books you are to receive from the Society, which were
at the late Mr. Somaster's house in the country, are after a
long delay arrived in town, and will come by Captain Miller,
by whom I propose also to send a parcel from the Bishop of
Oxford, which I have kept some time, expecting to deliver it
to you with my own hand, and Dart's "Antiquities of Canterbury," — a present, with his affectionate compliments,
from Dr. Berkeley, which he imagines may give you some
amusement.   The freight of the books is paid by the Society.

I have such a flow of company now I am getting better,

that I have little time allowed me to write, and must conclude with my tenderest love to all the family, and compliments to all friends, and am

Honored Sir, your most dutiful son and humble servant,

WM. SAML. JOHNSON.

He had so far recovered from his illness by the end of August as to take occasional rides into the country, and in September he made a brief visit to his friend, Dr. Berkeley, at Cookham. The excursion did him much good, but such were his anxieties about his family, and affairs in Connecticut, and such his fears of being misunderstood for tarrying in England, that he could not refrain from repeating them, and asking the candor of his friends for a favorable construction of his conduct till he could particularly explain to them the motives by which he had been influenced. Even before he made this visit, he wrote a letter to his son-in-law, Rev. Mr. Kneeland, which is too fine a picture of his affectionate heart, and personal sacrifice not to be spread upon these pages : —

WESTMINSTER, *Sept.* 8, 1770.

DEAR SIR, — I should long since have returned you my thanks for your obliging favor of February 23d, had I not, ever since I received it, been continually expecting a release from my tedious confinement in this country. The considerations you suggest to me, to hasten my return home, are of the most interesting and alarming nature, and have very long filled me with the most anxious solicitude. Even while I was every day almost expecting to embark for America, they gave me very deep concern ; but now that it seems doubtful whether I must not be detained here yet some few months longer (the reasons of which I have at large explained both to my father and to Mrs. Johnson), I own, they

almost overwhelm me with affliction, and I even tremble at
the danger which threatens me. All my felicity, in this
world, depends upon the felicity of my dear wife and family,
and that all, I see by your letter, now stands upon the brink
of a most dangerous precipice in most imminent hazard of
being lost. What a tremendous situation am I in! Cannot
you, my dear sir, interpose, and do something to prevent the
impending ruin? Have you no influence with my poor,
dear, distressed wife? If you have any, let me beg you will
exert it all. Persuade her to lay aside her anxieties and
cares, to resume her resolution and firmness, and to lengthen
out her patience and fortitude yet a little longer. The delays I have lately met with in my affairs have been inevitable, and the act of Providence alone. I have done all that
was possible. The Attorney General's illness, and my own,
have prevented the finishing of my business. Her patience
shall, certainly, be tried but a very little longer. The Mohegan cause cannot be postponed longer, at furthest, than
till about Christmas; but whether it be or not, at all events,
if God spares my life, I will come out early in the spring.
Nothing shall detain me beyond that period. Upon this
head my friends may speak with absolute certainty, nor will
I stay even so long as that, unless necessarily detained, and
by the best advice of my friends. Entreat her, then, to lay
aside every apprehension and anxiety, as all her troubles, as
far as depends on me, shall very soon have an end. Let her
give herself no concern at the confusion of my affairs, which
I am sensible the badness of the times, and the iniquity of
men, have very greatly embarrassed. It is too much for her
to give attention to them. Such of them as by assiduity and
attention can be retrieved, I will retrieve; such as cannot,
let them take their fate, they are not worth a thought in
comparison of her repose. To this let her give all her attention, and provide only for her present ease and quiet. She
has, I know, been too solicitous about my affairs, as well as
about me; would to God she would now be only solicitous
about herself, make herself and the children happy, and

leave to me the care of all the rest, who will take care of them, as far as care can be of any consequence. I can bear any loss with sufficient patience, but the loss of her, and the family's quiet and happiness. Let me beg you will exert yourself to the utmost upon this occasion, and pardon the earnestness with which I apply to you upon this most interesting subject, and impute it to the frankness with which you have opened yourself to me, which convinces me of your regard and solicitude for the family. As I shall remain in the most anxious state of solicitude, I beg you will write me by the first opportunity, and give me a full state of the family. Conceal nothing from me, for I always wish to know the worst, as well as the best, of things. Should it happen that I have left England before your letter arrives, as I certainly shall as soon as possible, I will leave directions that it may follow me back again to America. Your services upon this occasion will lay me under very lasting obligations.

There is very little, at this dull season of the year (when you know all the Boards of State are shut up, and most of the great people are amusing themselves in the country), worth telling you with respect to public affairs. The spirit of party is as violent as ever, but the opposition have rather lost ground ever since the beginning of the last spring. The Ministry of course appear to be very strong; indeed I apprehend they will be a good deal strengthened by the late measure adopted at New York, which they foretold, and which is at present the subject of much conversation; and is equally condemned by one party and approved by the other. Time will show us whether the consequences of it will be beneficial or detrimental.

The Parliamentary History (which my father tells me you inquired after) has not been brought down beyond the Restoration. The Debates in Parliament, which have been pretty regularly published since that period, and collected by Chandler and Grey, are considered as a sufficient continuation of that work. I inclose a letter to Mrs. Kneeland,

and with my best wishes for the continuance of your mutual felicity, remain,   Your very affectionate father

And humble servant,

WM. SAML. JOHNSON.

Confident that the Mohegan cause would be finished somehow in a short time, he resolved to be content with his situation, pass another winter in London, and watch the progress of political events. Writing to a friend in this country,[1] Dec. 29, 1770, he said: " The general American controversy is at present looked upon here as very much at an end. The Ministry are thought to have gained their point, and the Colonies to have submitted to be governed and disposed of in future in the manner they shall be pleased to direct. Is it so? Such certainly are the present appearances. I will make no reflections upon it, though very many are ready to start from my pen."

Johnson could see that the career of Lord North, the Prime Minister, was gaining for the time the public confidence; and his administration was strengthened by majorities in Parliament that did not shrink at the prospect of war with the united powers of France and Spain. Nothing, however, was stable. " The politics of this country are," said he, " like its climate, continually varying, and we know not what to expect." He was himself inclined to moderate measures on both sides, and opposed to violence. While unwilling to surrender the rights for which he had so long contended, he was fully satisfied, upon mature reflection and careful observation, that if the Colonies had consented to take upon themselves a

[1] Jeremiah Miller.

portion of the expenses of the old French War, and to
bear a share of the support of their Provincial Governments, " they might," to use his own words, uttered
in the calm of his declining years, " have made an
amicable arrangement with Great Britain, and continued with her until they would of course become
independent, and like ripe fruit have fallen from the
tree without any concussion or expenditure of blood
and treasure." Dr. Johnson " attended at the Cockpit the final hearing of the Mohegan cause," Tuesday
June 11, 1771, and if the result proved not entirely
in favor of the Colony, it certainly was not a victory
for the heirs of Mason. He made immediate preparations to return to America, and sought interviews
with those who had specially befriended him or been
the correspondents of his father. Bishop Lowth,
with whom he had conversed freely upon political
and religious subjects, addressed him the following
note : —

DEAR SIR, — I thought myself very unfortunate in miss-
ing of you before I left London, both at my house and yours,
and much more, when I found by your obliging note that
you are to leave England so soon. Had I been aware of
this I would have taken care to have made some appointment with you which might have succeeded better. I most
heartily wish you a safe voyage and all possible happiness in
America. I shall be extremely glad of the favor of your
correspondence, and any information of the state of affairs in
that country you may be sure will at all times be most acceptable to me.

If at any time I can be of any service to you in England
you will give me a real pleasure by employing me. I beg
you to present my sincerest respects to your good father ;
and with my best wishes both to him and yourself, and the

truest regard and esteem, I desire you would believe me to
be   .   Dear Sir, your most obedient and
                          Affectionate humble servant,
                                              R. OXFORD.
CUDDESDON, OXFORDSHIRE, *June* 29, 1771.

On the 12th of July he set out with Mr. Temple
for his last visit to Dr. Berkeley at Canterbury, and
took delight for three days in renewing the pleasant
acquaintances which he had previously made in that
place and neighborhood. For the remainder of his
stay in England he was occupied with matters of a
public and private nature ; and having discharged the
other trusts and responsibilities committed to him,
and taken leave of his many friends, he bade adieu to
London, and sailed from Gravesend for New York on
Saturday, the 3d of August, and at 7 o'clock in the
evening of the first day of the following October, he
was safe at his home in Stratford. After such a long
absence, what greetings awaited him ! Not only was
he welcomed by his family and by his aged father,
who had begun to feel that he might not live till his
return, but he was welcomed, cordially welcomed, by
his friends and neighbors and by the Colony of Connecticut.

The General Assembly, which was on the eve of
holding its autumn session, appointed a committee on
the 29th of October, to " return him their thanks for
his faithful service," while acting as their agent at
the Court of Great Britain, and to " testify their approbation of his constant endeavors to promote the
general cause of American liberty, and his steady
attention to the true interest of this Colony in particular." His answer to that committee has been

preserved, and is a part of his official and personal history: "I want words to express the deep sense I have of the honor the General Assembly have been pleased to confer upon me, and I beg you will assure them that I received it with the warmest gratitude. It was my duty, in the situation in which I had the honor to be placed in England, to give the most careful attention to the interests of American Liberty, and to the rights of the Colony of Connecticut; and I am extremely happy that my well-meant services have been in any degree acceptable to my fellow-citizens, for whose approbation and regard I have the highest value. I shall ever consider it as the great honor of my life to have had the thanks of the General Assembly; and they may rely upon it that while I live, I shall esteem it my duty to render every service in my power to the Colony of Connecticut, for which I have the highest respect and the most ardent affection."

CHAPTER VIII.

CONGRATULATIONS UPON HIS RETURN; DEATH OF HIS FATHER;
LETTERS FROM FRIENDS; APPOINTED JUDGE OF SUPERIOR
COURT; CHIEF JUSTICESHIP OF NEW YORK, AND FOREIGN
CORRESPONDENCE.

A. D. 1771–1773.

OF the many friends who welcomed his return to
America, no one was more hearty in his congratulation than Jared Ingersoll, his former associate at the
Bar, and the famous Stamp-master of Connecticut.
Probably no one could enter more thoroughly into
his feelings than he, or better understand the change
from London to Stratford. In responding to his welcome, Johnson wrote the following characteristic letter : —

October 28, 1771

DEAR SIR, — I very heartily thank you for your obliging
congratulations on my return to my native country, and sincerely rejoice with Mrs. Ingersoll and you in her recovery
from the unlucky consequences of the small-pox.

I miss you much here, and want to spend a long time with
you, but know not when this will be possible, as I think of
nothing else than returning to my old course of business ; and
even if I had not determined upon this, have enough to do
to bring my own affairs again into some order from the great
confusion they have unavoidably run into by my long absence, — an absence for which I can make no apology to Mrs.

Ingersoll, but, as I have hitherto done, throw myself absolutely upon the mercy of the ladies, hardly expecting at the same time perfect pardon.

Why do you, who should inform me, ask me how my situation will agree with me? You have twice made the transition from the gayety of London to the gloom of New Haven, — from the ease and indolence of the parlor and Coffee House, to the business and bustle of the Bar, and perfectly know the difference between living idly upon six hundred per annum, and working hard for two. You have felt all the sensations that those distant extremes can excite, and could, I dare say, represent them to me in strong colorings. To me all is new, and I can only say that I feel myself so happy, hitherto, in the enjoyment of my family and friends, that it seems as if nothing could ever again disconcert or be disagreeable to me. In this happy humor I shall at least enter upon the scene of business and of poverty which is before me with great alacrity, and, I dare say, shall sustain it with cheerfulness ; for I have long been resolved to be content with whatever Providence allots me. And after all what is the mighty difference between the rattles of the man and boy ? both are but toys, and if we are wise we shall be alike pleased with both. We cannot be very happy in any situation in this life: we may be tolerably so in almost any, if we make the best of it. " Some strong comfort," says our friend Pope very truly, " every state attends." But I have no leisure to philosophize. . . . .

A friend in Boston, Robert Temple, who had been his frequent companion during the first year of his sojourn in England, congratulated him in an earnest letter, which bears so directly upon the history of the times that it is produced here in full.

TEN HILLS, *January* 20, 1772.

DEAR JOHNSON, — I fully intended to have been in Connecticut last October, which is the reason why I have not before now welcomed you back to your own country, friends, and family, who I hope you found in good health — happy they could not be till your return. Why did you not comply with your promise ? You said you would return to New England in some of the many vessels belonging to Boston. I was much disappointed when I heard of your arrival at New York. I promised myself great pleasure in seeing you. I had rather have one evening's conversation with you about men and things in the great world (and I'm sure I should be better informed by it) than by reading all the papers that have been printed for four years past. And I will, if possible, contrive to see you before my ideas grow cold and stale. Pray, will your business or pleasure bring you as far as New London in the course of this winter? I have promised Godfrey Malbone a visit, and should be happy in seeing you. I am sorry we live at so great a distance from each other. Herewith I send you a packet and a single letter, which, with my letters, came in a trunk from my brother John, so that I did not receive them till this morning. Notwithstanding the weight and number of my brother's diabolical enemies, I am in no doubt but that he will very soon have a provision superior to what he was stripped of for being an honest man.

O Johnson, if there ever was a man whose Christianity has been put to the test, I am one, but as I have stood it out so long, I earnestly wish that I may not be obliged to break that solemn chain, which alone has hitherto kept me from doing one piece of justice to myself ; but enough of this. Pray, how does my friend Whately stand; in what box is he since the death of poor Mr. Grenville ? I can't account for not receiving a line from him for more than a year. I suppose he, as well as some other of my friends, have been impressed with an idea that I am a Son of Liberty — licentiousness, I mean. A son of true liberty I ever will be, as I think they are the only true friends to good government, and not the sly, designing crew who are reputed friends to government, when their only object and idol is power and

money, — two invincible and destructive powers, from which
God of His infinite mercy deliver me. You'll make me happy
by saying you intend a visit to Boston in next summer, and
I should be sorry to think it were necessary to tell you that
I and Mrs. Temple should have great pleasure in entertain-
ing you, Mrs. Johnson, or as many as might accompany you.
Ten Hills is large enough to accommodate horses, servants,
etc., and you'll find a hearty welcome.

Mrs. Temple and my girls join me in sincere regards to
Mrs. Johnson and your daughter Nancy.

I am with unfeigned regard, yours, etc.,

R. TEMPLE.[1]

His venerable father, who for more than half a
century had been a conspicuous and fearless actor in
the ecclesiastical and educational affairs of the Colonies, and who had scarcely finished his rejoicings at
the return of his son, died at Stratford on the morning of January 6, 1772. His exit, like that of Bishop
Berkeley, was without premonition to friends, seeming, as James Duane expressed it in a letter[2] to the
son, "more like the flight of Elijah to the mansions
of bliss than the melancholy departure of souls less
pure and innocent."

Among those in England to whom Johnson transmitted at once intelligence of this event was the Bishop
of Oxford, to whom he wrote a week after its occurrence, and having described its manner and interceded
for the appointment of his son-in-law, the Rev. Mr.
Kneeland, to the vacant mission at Stratford, he went
on to speak in a general way of colonial prospects and
interests. "This is, my lord," said he, "a great and
important part of his Majesty's dominions, every day
increasing at a most rapid rate, and which in every

---

[1] See Appendix B.   [2] Appendix C.

light demands the attention of all who wish the prosperity of the British Empire. To our political concerns I do not ask your lordship's attention further
than as a Lord of Parliament it will become you to
engage in them ; but I earnestly entreat your lordship's very particular attention to the interests of religion in this country, — the most important of all
others. Take the Church of England in the Colonies,
my lord, I beseech you, under your immediate pat-
ronage and protection. It is a noble field for the display of those admirable talents which your lordship
is blessed with. Much good may be done here by
supporting the cause of that excellent Church, which
no person can do so effectually as your lordship's
established reputation, particularly in the Colonies,
will enable you to do. It is a cause in which his late
Grace of Canterbury labored with great assiduity and
success. It has done honor to his name and memory,
and I doubt not is at this moment one occasion of
his joy and rejoicing."

Dr. Berkeley, to whom he had also made known
his bereavement, wrote him as follows, from

CANTERBURY, *March* 14, 1772.

MY DEAR FRIEND, — In my last, dated January 1, I told
you and your, alas, late ! excellent father, how happy we were
to hear of your mutual felicity, and how kindly Lord Dartmouth promised, if it comes in his way, to render you the
desired service. The public papers have now increased our
rejoicing at your arrival in Connecticut, time enough for that
good and amiable man to embrace his beloved son once more
in the foreign country of this world. God conduct us by
redeeming mercy to our own home, whither he whom we
lament is gone before in the faith of Jesus, — that faith which
has never been assaulted with quite so much fury in this

Island as in the present winter. At Oxford the distress is
not small on account of Sir William Meredyth's notice that
he will bring in, and it is feared successfully, a bill to set
aside all subscription to the Articles of our faith, either at
matriculation or at admission to degrees. Sir William is the
tool, and a very ignorant one, of an impious wretch, one
Priestley, a Dissenting minister, who, *in terminis*, has taxed
our Church with idolatry for worshipping that Saviour whom
all the angels of heaven incessantly adore. Mr. Trecothick
has been persuaded by Sir William, his brother-in-law, to
take part against the Church of England. Dr. Nowell of
Oxford has given great handle to the enemies of our University, to abuse it as a seminary of slavish principles. His
sermon, written in defiance of all history, and with no small
rancor, has been most deservedly censured by the House of
Commons. Sir Fletcher had drawn the House in to thank
the Doctor for his doctrine and to request its publication,
but there has been a subsequent order for expunging the
thanks, and Nowell is lucky that the enraged members
stopped there. . . . .

In another letter, dated April 4, Robert Temple
referred to his own uneasiness at the spirit of the
times, and spoke in triumph of the provision which
had been made for his brother in England. An extract will furnish an interesting page of family history : —

You justly observe, a day is coming when all things will
be adjusted, and experience proves that a steady perseverance in an honest course does sometimes, even in this cor-
rupt state, procure for us a redress of grievances.

I flatter myself you will be pleased in hearing that my
brother is provided for. He is appointed Surveyor General
of the Customs in England. The establishment is £400 per
annum, and 40*s.* per day for travelling expenses. In addition to this my brother has a standing warrant for £300 per

annum during the time he may hold that place; so that con-
sidering the iniquitous weight that was against him, and that
his friends were not in administration, I think he has discovered some generalship in keeping the field against such a
diabolical force, — some of whom, for these six months, have
been predicting that my brother would be cast off, if not
exchequered, and these pretty fellows even now pretend to
disbelieve or vilify his appointment. But you may be assured that what I write is fact. My brother has ordered all
his effects in this country to be disposed of. His wife and
family will embark for England in three weeks. This, I
fear, is his final farewell to his native country, for which he
has the warmest affection. But as acquiescence is the indispensable duty of us mortals, I can only say in this, as in all,
the will of Heaven be done.

When I wrote you last I had not heard that your good,
venerable father had ceased from his labors and was gone to
rest. God grant that we may perform the troublesome,
though short journey of life with his reputation; if so, we
may be permitted to take our leave of this lower world in
that joyful hope that I trust he did.

Bishop Lowth, in answer to the letter written on
the 13th of January, said : —

DEAR SIR, — The news of the death of your good father
had reached me before I received the favor of your letter.
He died in a good old age; without pain; retaining his intellectual faculties to the last; having finished an useful and
exemplary life with great credit and reputation; full of hope,
and ripe for the joys of heaven, —

> "it is a consummation
> Devoutly to be wished!"

I will not therefore attempt to do a thing really so improper
as to condole with you on this occasion.

Dr. Burton had likewise communicated to me beforehand
your wishes in regard to Mr. Kneeland; and I had concurred

with him in thinking it a matter which we might with great propriety promote, when it shall be proposed to the Society. I was at the last meeting, when this and the other particular which you requested were proposed. Though both somewhat out of the common course, they were passed without doubt or hesitation in any one present; or rather with an unanimous zeal, by which every one was ready to testify their regard to the memory of the late worthy Dr. Johnson.

You do me the honor to expect much more from me than I can possibly perform in the service of the public. My honest zeal and my best endeavors you may depend upon. You will do me great pleasure and great service, if you will be so good as to favor me with your correspondence; and inform me at any time in regard to any matters on your side of the Atlantic, which it may be expedient that we should perfectly know and rightly understand here.

With my best wishes for your health and happiness,

I am, dear sir,

Your most obedient humble servant,

R. OXFORD.

DUKE STREET, WESTMINSTER, *May* 18, 1772.

Dr. Johnson resumed his place in the Upper House of the General Assembly, and at its May session, 1772, was appointed one of the Judges of the Superior Court. Dr. Dwight, President of Yale College, described his gifted sire as "the father of Episcopacy in Connecticut." In some such sense, Dr. Johnson was the father of the Bar in Connecticut; for, as already mentioned, he threw new light into the chambers of equity by citing legal decisions and doctrines of civilians which were comparatively unknown to the great body of the profession.

Richard Stockton, a signer of the Declaration of Independence, writing him on the 18th of February, 1773, said: "I congratulate you, or rather the Colony of Connecticut, on your appointment to a seat on the Bench of your Superior Court, which I was informed of by the gentleman who brought me your last letter. It is not ordinarily so profitable in this country as the crawling Bar ; but it is more easy and dignified ; and it has the advantage of an argument much more weighty with you than either of these, — the doing good."

His name had been mentioned for the Chief Justiceship of New York when it should become vacant, and men of influence and high standing had interceded for him to be appointed to the place, even before he took his departure from England. The Bishop of London (Terrick) commended him highly to Lord Hillsborough, then in power, and at the same time expressed his earnest wishes that a person might not succeed to that office whose prejudices were strong against the Established Church. His fast friend, Dr. Berkeley, who was disposed to serve him in every way, and had withal such a desire to see a bishop in America as to be ready himself to assume the responsibilities, wrote him the following characteristic letter, from

CANTERBURY, 19th *October*, 1772.

MY DEAR FRIEND, — Although I have not heard from you since I last wrote on the subject of your son-in-law's affair, yet I will not deny myself the pleasure of congratulating America and you on Lord Dartmouth's acceptance of his present high office. I have very strongly recommended you to that most excellent nobleman, and I am persuaded he is disposed to listen to any proposal in your favor. I wish you to write a letter of congratulation to him, if you have not already done it, in which you may hint your hope of having the honor to serve his Majesty as Chief Justice of

New York. If you ever fancy that I can serve you, command me without ceremony. I shall not ask any favor for myself, unless peradventure an American mitre *in nubibus*, and I shall therefore be quite at liberty to use my little influence with Lord Dartmouth for the dear friend to whom I write. Tell me how a book can be conveyed to you.

I am just returned to this place for the winter. My mother and wife and children all well, I bless God. Public affairs are much as when your left us, except that Lord North has increased in personal weight ; this increase some knowing persons consider as a presage of ministerial dissolution. In this reign, a minister ought to have a certain measure of insignificance. Seriously turn it over in your mind whether an application could not be obtained from some Assembly in your new world for an American Bishop, — a Bishop who by law should be incapacitated from accepting a Bishopric in England or Ireland. My preferments here would furnish me with two, if not three active friends ; the American Secretary of State is really such to me, and I should rejoice to devote my life to the service of the Episcopal interest in America. I think aloud on this subject to you, and I beg of you not to publish needlessly my thoughts. If you choose to write to me on this or on any other subject very freely, add " Private " on the top of your page. Any letters not so marked, I shall understand to be meant for the inspection of Lord Dartmouth, and any other considerable man to whom you would wish to communicate American notices. I shall always reckon that day an happy one which brings me a letter full of good news from my dear Doctor Johnson.

Pray let me have your sentiments about the new settlement at Fort Pitt. Would not that be a good place wherein to obtain lands as an estate for my grandchildren? Let me have your advice on this point.

The motley crew of Deists, Socinians, Arians, etc., at the Feathers Tavern, threaten over their punch-bowl to demolish what is founded on a rock. Dr. Owen, Rector of St. Olave, Hart Street, in London, went to that Tavern in order to form an accurate judgment of the system there patronized, but those anti-subscribing gentry refused to give him any information as to their design until he should first have subscribed to their association.

I have just now had a severe, indeed irreparable loss, in the death of Mr. Monck of Dublin, my near relation and powerful friend. . . . .

Bishop Lowth was particularly interested for his advancement to the office of Chief Justice of New York. Johnson had written to him and reminded him of the favorable attention given to the matter by Lord Hillsborough during his administration, adding, " The office is now [October 31, 1772] held by a very old gentleman, already almost totally incapable of any business, and must, therefore, very soon be given to somebody. It is an office which I probably could and certainly would most assiduously labor to exercise to the honor of his Majesty's government and to the emolument of his subjects."

To this letter, in which were renewed also the importunities before made relative to the American Episcopate, the Bishop replied as follows : —

DEAR SIR, — I took the first opportunity that offered on my coming to town this year, of speaking to Lord Dartmouth, according to your desire. I had not entered very far into the subject, when his lordship in a manner prevented my proceeding, by telling me, that application had been made to him in your favor; that he knew you personally himself, and was very well inclined to serve you. I nevertheless thought it proper to enlarge a little upon what he might not have had opportunity of being so well assured of, and which in this case seemed to me of principal importance ; namely, your sincere affection and steady attachment to the government and the interests of this country, and the interests of the Colonies, as closely and necessarily connected with it. It gave me great pleasure to find this affair in so good a train.

As to the important object of our wishes, the American Episcopate, I think I see it still at as great a distance as ever. I do not doubt that excellent person would be very well inclined to it, if a fair opportunity of promoting it should offer; but in general the Ministry seem determined to put a stop to every motion of this kind, that may lead to any alteration in ecclesiastical matters, or may hazard the least disturbance. You may be assured that it is not in our power to do anything in it. Matters must be prepared on your side: nothing less than a strong and well-supported application from the Colonies, in general, or at least from the principal Colonies, will have any effect.

I have the honor to be with the greatest regard, dear sir,

Your most obedient humble servant,

R. OXFORD.

DUKE STREET, WESTMINSTER, *May 20, 1773.*

It would not be possible to introduce all his foreign correspondence at this period, without overloading these pages. For the most part it bears upon the same general topics, and is a repetition of the common concern felt for the relations of the Colonies to the mother country. The two letters which follow have a literary value that entitles them to be re-printed[1] in this connection. If others passed between the two great men, they are not now to be found, and the approach of the Revolution may have suddenly terminated the correspondence.

To DR. JOHNSON.

SIR, — Of all those whom the various accidents of life have brought within my notice, there is scarce any one

[1] See *Life and Correspondence of Samuel Johnson, D. D.,* pp. 361–365.

whose acquaintance I have more desired to cultivate than yours. I cannot, indeed, charge you with neglecting me, yet our mutual inclination could scarce gratify itself with opportunities; the current of the day always bore us away from one another, and now the Atlantic is between us.

Whether you carried away an impression of me as pleasing as that which you left me of yourself, I know not; if you did, you have not forgotten me, and will be glad that I do not forget you. Merely to be remembered is indeed a barren pleasure, but it is one of the pleasures which is more sensibly felt as human nature is more exalted.

To make you wish that I should have you in my mind, I would be glad to tell you something which you do not know; but all public affairs are printed, and as you and I had no common friends, I can tell you no private history.

The government, I think, grows stronger, but I am afraid the next general election will be a time of uncommon turbulence, violence, and outrage.

Of literature no great product has appeared, or is expected; the attention of the people has for some years been otherwise employed.

I was told two days ago of a design which must excite some curiosity. Two ships are [in] preparation, which are under the command of Captain Constantine Phipps, to explore the Northern Ocean; not to seek the northeast or the northwest passage, but to sail directly north, as near the pole as they can go. They hope to find an open ocean, but I suspect it is one mass of perpetual congelation. I do not much wish well to discoveries, for I am always afraid they will end in conquest and robbery.

I have been out of order this winter, but am grown better. Can I ever hope to see you again; or must I be always content to tell you that in another hemisphere, I am, Sir,

Your most humble servant,

SAMUEL JOHNSON.

JOHNSON'S COURT, FLEET STREET, LONDON, *March* 4, 1773.

STRATFORD, *June* 5, 1773.

DEAR AND RESPECTED SIR, — I am perfectly unable to express the grateful sense I have of the singular honor you have done me by your favor of the 4th of March. There was no man in England whose acquaintance I so much wished to be honored with when I first embarked in my late voyage. Your excellent writings had given me the highest veneration and esteem of your character. I waited some time for some accidental or favorable introduction to you, but when none offered, I presumed so much on the idea I had formed of you, that I at last ventured to introduce myself to you in the abrupt manner you remember. The kind and obliging reception you then, and ever after gave me, when I waited upon you, confirmed and increased my respect, and your kind remembrance of me now lays me under such obligations as I must never hope to repay. To be remembered by one of the first characters of an age, in which there are so few whose remembrance is not rather a reproach than an honor, is, I assure you, to me one of the highest pleasures that I am capable of.

I bless God that at the date of your letter, you were returning again to health, which I hope will be very long continued to you not only for your own sake, but of human nature, which will be benefited by your labors, for you live not for yourself, but for all mankind.

It will, I hope, be some satisfaction to you to know that your writings are in the highest esteem, and are doing much good in this extensive and growing country, and will, I doubt not, continue to do so to very late posterity; for which reason, as well as for the increase of your reputation, which I assure you is very dear to me, I hope you will be still preparing something for the public, who will read with the utmost avidity whatever appears under the sanction of your name.

It gives me great pleasure to learn from so good an authority, that government grows stronger. You had indeed convinced me that the alarm which the factious and the desperate had excited was false, but I hardly expected when I left England, that government would have obtained so speedy and so manifest a superiority over the friends of confusion, as, if we may credit the printed accounts, it seems to have done. From them it would seem as if the cause of opposition was almost desperate. It must be expected, however, that every effort will be made to revive it against the next general election, and I wish your apprehensions may not be verified; but still I hope there is no great danger of their gaining so great advantages as to enable them to do much mischief to the public. Upon the stability of government will depend, also, in a high degree, the felicity of this country. The government have much to do here, where the opinion that has been maintained by the Boston Assembly [in] a late dispute with no opposition to their governor, that the Colonies are independent of the Parliament of Great Britain, gains ground, and will require their attention, unless they mean to acquiesce in the idea, and give up their authority over us, which I presume they will not be inclined to do.

The design you mention of exploring the Northern Ocean is an experiment of great curiosity, and I shall be impatient to know the success of it. I have ever entertained the opinion you seem to have adopted, that the Pole is the empire of frost and snow, which will effectually forever stop the gains from those evils, which, as you justly remark, have generally been the consequence of discoveries. Neither ambition nor avarice, I fancy, will there have an opportunity for gratification; we shall only acquire an innocent, and perhaps useless acquaintance with an unknown part of our globe.

I wish I could gratify you with any intelligence from this side of the Atlantic; but nothing occurs to me worthy of your notice. I have lost since my return to America my venerable father, who, to his other good qualities, added a sincere respect and esteem for you, and was extremely minute and particular in his inquiries concerning you. We had the happiness to spend three months together after my return, when he expired full of days, satisfied with life, with hopes full of immortality, and without a groan or any apparent previous pain.

For myself I am again engaged largely in the busy, and in this country not very profitable, profession of the law, which, however, answers tolerably well for the support of the numerous young family with which God has blessed me. That you may enjoy every felicity, and long, very long, continue as you have done to bless mankind, be useful to the world, is and will be the sincere and ardent prayer of, dear sir,

Your most obedient and most faithful humble servant,

WM. SAMUEL JOHNSON.

To Dr. SAMUEL JOHNSON,
Johnson's Court, Fleet Street, London.

CHAPTER IX.

A. D. 1773–1779.

THE Parliamentary measures in reference to the
American Colonies did not quiet the apprehensions
of the people. The proposition of Lord North, to
repeal all duties except that upon tea, was unsatis-
factory, and the popular discontent manifested itself
principally in Massachusetts, where the local authorities were brought into frequent conflict with the officers of the crown. In vain did Benjamin Franklin,
then residing in London as an agent for several of
the Colonies, acquaint British ministers with the true
state of things in this country, and assure them that
combined resistance would follow an attempt to enforce laws which deprived the American people of
their just rights. He had been in England now this
second time many years; was there prior to the passage of the Stamp Act; and Johnson had often conferred with him and been always ready to join his
own voice to his in pleading for a magnanimous
policy towards the Colonies.

An immense quantity of tea lay stored in the warehouses of the East India Company in England, and cargoes of it were shipped to agents at Boston, New York, and other places, upon which a duty of three pence per pound was to be paid, not so much apparently to raise a revenue as to assert the right of Parliamentary taxation. It was a decisive moment for the Colonies, and while the resistance elsewhere was more moderate, at Boston violent opposition was made to the landing of the tea, and a body of men in the disguise of Indians went on board the ships, and in less than two hours three hundred and forty chests were broken and thrown into the harbor. The colonial authorities were powerless to prevent the disorder. It was evident that the public senti-ment of America was becoming embittered, and the course pursued by the home government was not calculated to allay the irritation. For the British Ministry, on hearing of these occurrences, determined not to yield the point in dispute, but, as Lord North said, " to take such vigorous steps as shall ultimately persuade the Americans that England has not only the power, but also the will, to maintain them in obedience ; in a word, that she is unalterably deter-mined to protect her laws, her commerce, her mag-istrates, and her own dignity."

Thus the political events in both countries were shaping towards a Revolution, and filling Johnson, as they filled others, with much anxiety. Dr. Berke-ley, who had kept him well informed of the drift of things in England since his return, and especially of propositions that bore upon the religious interests of the Colonies, foreshadowed his own fears and the attempts to compel submission, which he believed would be successful, in a letter dated,—

RAMSGATE IN THANET, *August* 11, 1774.

MY DEAR FRIEND,—In my last letter to you, dated at Cookham, February 3, 1774, I returned you my hearty thanks for your kind present of Newtown Pippins,—a cask of which was forwarded to me at my parish, where I and my family spent the winter. My mother has had very much illness and has been kept alive with great difficulty. I bless God she is now better than she has been for many months, and my wife and children and Miss Frinsham are well, and very much your true friends.

I have suffered greatly in my own mind on American affairs. I see nothing but clouds in the American sky, and I feel unfeignedly for that country, to which I bear an hereditary love. Poor Mr. Temple[1] has caused me no small share of additional concern, and I can hardly form an idea of a more miserable man than he now is. He has spent near six months at my friend Mr. Lance's. I wish I could speak a word of comfort to you, my much loved friend, on

---

[1] JOHN TEMPLE. Certain letters written by Governor Hutchinson and others to Thomas Whately, a member of Parliament, though not official but intended to affect public measures, had been printed in Boston and copies transmitted to London. Curiosity was at once excited to know by whom the original letters were sent over to this country. Thomas Whately was dead, and his papers had passed into the possession of his brother William, who had allowed Mr. Temple to examine them for the purpose of finding a certain document in relation to the Colonies. He now suspected Mr. Temple of having taken advantage of the permission to acquire the letters in question, and a duel between them ensued in which Mr. Whately was wounded. Dr. Franklin, still in London, immediately published a declaration in which he assumed the whole responsibility of having transmitted the original letters, and said, "that as they were not among Mr. Thomas Whately's papers when these passed into the hands of his brother, neither he nor Mr. Temple could have been concerned in withdrawing them."

The unhappiness referred to in Dr. Berkeley's letter must have been the result of this occurrence.

public affairs. If I could, believe me I should have wrote
to you often since February. Administration is determined,
as I believe, to carry every point, in every part of North
America. It is almost universally supposed here that your
resolutions against importing our manufactures will be vio-
lated by a great majority of the subscribers. If so, the
English manufacturers will not plead your cause. Those
gentlemen here who have no immediate enjoyment or near
expectation of ministerial loaves and fishes, are I believe
generally dissatisfied with the Quebec Bill, and the middle
and lower ranks seem not to care about it. I need not to
tell you that this country is very far gone in a spirit of *Gal-
lionism:* so that matters merely religious are in general but
coolly attended to. I believe, and it is generally understood, that Lord Dartmouth was overruled in the Cabinet
on some important questions relative to the Quebec Bill;
the adopting English criminal law in that Province was,
I apprehend, solely at his instance. The change in one
of the late American Bills, subjecting persons accused of
crimes, alleged to be committed in America, to a removal
for trial to England at the will of the Governor, is extremely
odious to the unprejudiced part of the people of the island.
If I was retained at present, as an American advocate, I
would dwell very much on that arbitrary clause. I do suppose that it is resolved to support the claim of power to
raise a revenue in America, and I do suppose that any long-
continued and consistent abstinence from importation would
drive the Ministry to their wits' end. If the Americans have
public virtue enough to carry this scheme into execution,
they may carry several material points ; but I verily believe
that the servants of the government judge rightly as to the
improbability of such an event. Administration might and
ought to have placed a Protestant Bishop at Montreal, if
they had ever meant to place one of that order in North
America. This I am verily persuaded they never will do,
though Lord Dartmouth wishes it sincerely. I hope that
your duty, or your ideas of duty, may not draw you, my

dear friend, into any scrape; if you are so involved, may
God extricate you. Pray send me word (and the name
shall be secret) whether the Episcopalian party differs from
other parties on the present dissensions? The great encouragement given to the Popish colony of Quebec was in all
probability given chiefly by way of creating a counterbal-
ance to the Protestant colonies.

England and its great men are just as they were when
you left *it* and *them*. The clergy who believe and who
preach the established doctrines are just as much caressed
by their superiors as when you were in England. The defence of established evangelical doctrines is determined on
by Administration. Therefore they must be defended in
the lump, even by those who disbelieve them, and who oppose them in the pulpit one by one. The avowed, alias the
honest, sincere enemies of the doctrines of our Church, are
almost as much disregarded by some great men as the honest and sincere friend of those doctrines. If Hoadly was
now alive and beginning the world, he would print in defence of the Thirty-nine Articles and preach against them,
or at least talk against them. I pray Jesus Christ to defend
my dear friend and all his family. I can never forget, or
cease to love you. Adieu.

On the 5th of September, nearly a month after the
date of the foregoing letter, a general Congress of
the Colonies met at Philadelphia to consult together
and devise measures for their mutual protection from
the arbitrary acts of the British Parliament. Johnson was one of the three first chosen to represent
Connecticut in that Congress, but having previously
accepted an appointment as arbitrator on the estate
of Van Rensselaer, of Albany, he was excused from
serving and his place was taken by Silas Deane. This
combination of Colonial Councils threatened a new
order of things, and was regarded in England by the

Parliamentary party as an audacious movement to excite the spirit of innovation and shake off the restraints of authority.

The Battle of Lexington on the 19th of April, 1775, threw the country into the greatest consternation, and several of the Colonial Legislatures immediately assembled, and among them that of Connecticut. It was proposed, not however by Johnson, who was still a member of the Council, but by some one else, that a deputation or committee should be sent to General Gage, then in command of the British forces at Boston, with a letter from the Governor of the Colony, the object of which was to stay hostile proceedings and inquire if some means could not be adopted to secure peace.

Johnson, though strongly opposed to engaging in this embassy, was compelled by the unanimous voice of the Assembly to enter upon it, and with him was associated Mr. Erastus Wolcott, a member of the Lower House. The identical instrument, with the broad seal of the Colony, and in the clear calligraphy of George Wyllys, Secretary, under the authority of which they proceeded with all dispatch to Boston, is still preserved. It reads thus:—

At a General Assembly of the Governor and Company of the English Colony of Connecticut in New England in America, holden at Hartford in said Colony (by special order of the Governor) on Wednesday, the twenty-sixth day of April, Anno Domini 1775:—

Resolved, By this Assembly, that William Samuel Johnson and Erastus Wolcott, Esq'rs, wait upon his Excellency Governor Gage, with the Letter written to him by his Honor our Governor, by the desire of this Assembly, and confer

with him on the subject contained in said Letter and request
his answer.

When they reached Enfield they met a part of
the Massachusetts delegates on their way to attend
the second Continental Congress in Philadelphia, and
found them warm and zealous in the cause of the
Colonies, and one of them even rejoicing that hostilities had commenced. At Springfield they fell in
with John Adams, another delegate, who stopped at
the same tavern, and the evening was passed in serious conversation on the critical affairs of the country.
Arriving at Charlestown, they found a British gun-
ship moored in the channel and no person allowed
to enter the town of Boston. But on learning their
errand the commander immediately sent his barge
to convey them over ; and now again they were perplexed, for the city appeared to be deserted ; no one
was to be seen in the streets, and they could not have
found General Gage had they not fortunately met an
English officer, Major Monchief, previously known to
Dr. Johnson at New York, who requested him to conduct and introduce them to his Excellency.

Upon being admitted into his presence, and deliv-
ering their letter, he expressed himself highly pleased
with their mission and strongly in favor of peace and
reconciliation, and receiving in a day or two his official answer, they returned to Charlestown and called
for their horses. No reply was made by the inn-
keeper, neither were their horses produced after repeated inquiry, nor any reason assigned for their
detention. But very soon the sheriff of the county
appeared and summoned them to accompany him to

the Convention of Massachusetts, which was assembled in the neighborhood, and there the Speaker
or President inquired of them who they were and
where they had been? "I replied," says Johnson,
"stating the transactions of our Assembly, and that
we, as a Committee from our Legislature, had with a
letter waited on General Gage, who had expressed
himself to us as very friendly to the suggestion, and
desirous of putting an end, if possible, to all the difficulties which had originated in this country, and
of coöperating, and exerting his own power to bring
about this result. And he had given us a letter to
our Legislature which I presumed — for I knew not
the contents — expressed those ideas, and this I produced and held in my hand." "Open that letter,"
said the Speaker, "and read it." Johnson presented
the letter to him and said : "It is not for me to open
this letter, nor will I; but as we are in your power,
you may open it if you please and think you have a
right to do so," at the same time reminding him that
Connecticut was independent of Massachusetts and
had the liberty to adopt her own measures. Upon
this they were ordered to retire, still in the custody
of the sheriff, and after an hour or two they were
called in again, the letter redelivered, and their
journey homeward no longer obstructed.[1]

Dr. Johnson parted with Mr. Wolcott at Windsor,
the place of his residence, and went alone into Hart-

---

[1] This narrative differs *toto cælo* from the briefer mention of the same
mission by Bancroft, *History of United States*, vol. vii. p. 321; and the
difference must be accounted for on the supposition that he relied for his
authority on some traditional testimony, and never knew of or had in his
hands the authentic manuscript from which the facts now given have
been drawn. See Appendix D.

ford, where he found that the General Assembly had risen, and, instead of leaving any directions for the Committee, or saying anything about their report, had adopted resolutions of a very contrary nature and tendency, and voted men and money for the war. This sudden change was effected through the instrumentality of the Massachusetts delegation.

John Adams wrote to his wife from Hartford, April 30th, saying : —

The Assembly of this Colony is now sitting at Hartford. We are treated with great tenderness, sympathy, friendship, and respect. Everything is doing by this Colony that can be done by men, both for New York and Boston. Keep your spirits composed and calm, and don't suffer yourself to be disturbed by idle reports and frivolous alarms. We shall see better times yet. Lord North is insuring us success.[1]

Finding himself thus deserted he returned solitarily to his home in Stratford; and retiring from the Council after the Declaration of Independence, he set himself quietly down to his studies, persuaded that he could not conscientiously join in a war against England, the abundance of whose resources and the feelings of whose people he knew so well, much less in a war against his own country.

But moderation and neutrality did not prolong the quiet he desired. In midsummer, 1779, after General Tryon made his expeditions into Connecticut, burnt Fairfield and Norwalk, and withdrew his troops on Long Island, the air was filled with rumors that he was preparing to return and destroy other towns on the coast, and especially Stratford. The inhab-

[1] *Letters*, vol. i. p. 36.

itants of that place were stricken with terror; and
leading gentlemen waited on Johnson, and knowing
him to be well acquainted with the British General,
insisted that he should seek an interview with him
and endeavor to dissuade him from burning the town.
He told them it was an idle proposition; that he was
fully convinced whatever purpose of this kind had
been formed, if any, would be executed, and, therefore, he declined to undertake the perilous mission.
A town meeting was called, and resolutions passed
that he should go, and a committee was appointed
to accompany him. As it was not a time to disobey
the voice of the people, he finally assented, not, however, without taking precautions to be clearly understood by his fellow-townsmen and protected from
insult or injury in person or property. A subscription paper was circulated about the place, drawn up
by Johnson and worded as follows : —

We, the subscribers, being exceedingly desirous, if possible, to save the town from the destruction it is now threatened with by the invasion of the British fleet and army, do
hereby request and desire Doctor William Samuel Johnson,
Captain Philip Nichols, Captain George Benjamin, and Mr.
Ebenezer Allen to use their influence, either in person or
by letter, with the British Admiral and General to save the
town. And we do hereby promise and most sacredly engage
to support them in the execution of their design, and to protect and defend them from any insult, injury, or abuse, either
in their persons, properties, or families, on account of their
making such application : as witness our hands this 12th day
of July, 1779.

Intelligence of this movement was communicated
to Oliver Wolcott, Major-General, with head-quarters

8

at Horseneck, and Lieutenant Colonel Jonathan Dimon was immediately sent to Stratford, before the
mission had been entered upon, to examine into the
commotion and disquiet there, and report the result.
He summoned before him the draughtsman of the
subscription paper, and several of the signers, "with
others of suspicious character," and found the whole
intent to be — first, to take the sense of the people,
in writing, whether any entreaty should be made to
spare the town or not, and then to secure the persons
and property of the appointed agents from insult and
injury. Though Dr. Johnson's words on the occasion
of that examination " were smoother than oil, yet they
were very swords " to his political enemies, and Colonel Dimon's report to General Wolcott brought back
from that officer this severe and unexpected order,
dated July 18 : —

SIR, — Your favor of yesterday is received. I shall make
no observations upon the tendency, or rather the conclusive
effect of those men's conduct who could wish to supplicate
the clemency of an enemy whose unparalleled barbarity has
put a dishonor upon human nature. To a mind enlightened
by science, and which views acts with their consequences, it
is impossible that it should not comprehend that the step
which was intended to be taken must, by inevitable consequences, involve in it the most abject submission to a tyranny
rendered, if possible, ten times more detestable than it was
before, by the very means by which it was designed to be
established. These are times when the usual forms of proceeding are to give place to a regard for the public safety,
and the love of country is to be preferred at all times to the
friendship of youth.

You are, therefore, Sir, directed to send, under guard or
otherwise, Dr. William Samuel Johnson, of Stratford, to the

town of Farmington, and deliver him to the care and custody of the civil authority of that town, and request of
them that they would secure or keep him under such proper
restraints as to prevent his having any correspondence with
the enemy.

A detachment of troops was sent to carry out this
order, and Johnson was made a prisoner, — but con-
scious of his innocence, and wishing to avoid a public
disturbance, he persuaded the officer to accept his
word of honor that he would proceed at once to
Farmington, and place himself voluntarily in the
custody of the selectmen. One of that board was
John Treadwell, an acquaintance of his, who declared,
after consultation with his colleagues, that they had
no business with him, and that if they put him under any restraint it would be a false imprisonment.
Johnson said he knew this, but suggested that, for
their sakes and his, it was necessary that they should
do something; and accordingly he proposed, as their
best course, that they should permit him to pass to
the Governor and Council of Safety, in whose hands
at that time was lodged the military authority of the
Colony, and whose decision alone would quiet the
people. Here is a copy of his parole, which tells the
story : —

FARMINGTON, July 23, A. D. 1779.

I, the subscriber, having been sent by order from Major
General Oliver Wolcott, as a prisoner to the care of the civil
authority of the town of Farmington, and by them permitted to go from thence to Lebanon on business with his
Excellency the Governor and Council of Safety, do pass my
word that on said journey and business I will do nothing
directly or indirectly against the interest and welfare of the

United States ; and that, on my having accomplished said
business, will return and put myself under the immediate
care of said authority, unless his Excellency the Governor
and Council of Safety, or his Excellency the Governor only,
shall direct otherwise.   WM. SAMUEL JOHNSON.

Having thus given his parole and received his pass,
he started on his solitary journey, and arriving at
Norwich, where the Council of Safety sat, unluckily
found that body not in session. But he proceeded
to Lebanon, the residence of Governor Trumbull, and
stated his condition and the object of his appearing
in his presence. As his Excellency knew his character well, and the principles on which he had acted
from the beginning of the war, it did not require any
urgent entreaty to enlist his sympathy and gain his
favor. He informed Dr. Johnson that the Council
would meet again in two days, when he could appear,
and the matter would be laid before them, and the
result communicated. The Council met, and his own
statement went to show that he had no inclination to
aid the enemy; that he had encouraged the enlist-
ment of soldiers ; contributed of his property for that
purpose, hired his man to serve for him during the
war, and was ready to take the oath of fidelity required by law.

After hearing the case, his Excellency the Governor was advised to permit him, until further orders,
to return and remain in Stratford, which he speedily
reached to the great joy of his family and friends,
whose anxiety during his brief absence had been pain-
fully excited.

He was left to his own quietude after this, and no
attempt was again made to put him in a position

which he refused to occupy. His books were his chief companions, and there is a perfect blank in his correspondence at this period. When it became evident that the war must terminate in favor of the independence of the Colonies, he resumed the practice of his profession, and some time subsequent to the declaration of peace was reinstated in his old office as a member of the Upper House of the General Assembly.

CHAPTER X.

TRIAL OF THE SUSQUEHANNA CASE; CHOSEN A DELEGATE IN
CONGRESS; LETTER FROM HIS COLLEAGUE; FEARFUL TIMES;
SHAYS'S INSURRECTION; CONVENTION OF DELEGATES FROM ALL
THE STATES, AND FEDERAL CONSTITUTION.

A. D. 1779–1787.

THE return to the practice of his profession was
followed by a steady influx of business. Several of his
compeers at the bar had passed away. The Revolution had closed the duties of Jared Ingersoll, and he
had died in New Haven at the age of fifty-nine,
while other friends who contemplated separation from
England with untold affliction had fled to the British
Provinces for protection and personal safety. Johnson, however, had been too well known in New York
and in the courts of Connecticut to be without clients,
and his general intelligence and conservative spirit
in political matters made him a valuable adviser
upon questions that grew out of the state of the
times.

Towards the end of the year 1782, he was one
of the three counselors for Connecticut — Colonel
Eliphalet Dyer and Jesse Root were the other two
— in the trial of what was known as the great Susquehanna case. This was a controversy between
Connecticut and Pennsylvania about the jurisdiction

and proprietorship of the lands in the valley of Wyoming. Hundreds of emigrants from Connecticut had poured into that beautiful valley, and acquired rights, through the Susquehanna Company, which they appealed to their own State to vindicate in opposition to the claim of the successors of William Penn.

Provision had been made in the Articles of Confederation for the adjustment of any difficulties that might arise between the States, and as Connecticut, after the Revolution, continued to assert the jurisdiction which she had so long exercised over the Wyoming settlements, Pennsylvania was forced to apply to Congress for the appointment of a commission to hear the parties in interest and decide the question of proprietorship. Accordingly commissioners were appointed, who met at Trenton, New Jersey; and after a weary trial of five weeks' duration, they came to the unanimous conclusion, on the 30th day of December, that Connecticut had no right to the territory in dispute, and that the jurisdiction and preëmption of all the lands within her chartered limits belonged to Pennsylvania.

Dr. Johnson was disappointed at this result, and was so fully convinced of the right of Connecticut in the case that he declared the decision must have been in her favor had the commission been composed of able lawyers to determine the question. The people of Wyoming were at first indifferent to the result, supposing that it had reference only to the matter of jurisdiction, and that they might as well render allegiance to Pennsylvania as to Connecticut, provided they were left to the quiet possession and enjoyment

of their farms. But a day soon came which opened
their eyes to new horrors, and they found themselves
under masters whose tender mercies did not forbid
them to adopt measures tantamount to a compulsion
of the settlers to relinquish their lands and improvements, which had been purchased by untold sufferings and consecrated by the blood of their kindred.
This is not the place, however, to go into a recital
of subsequent acts. The muse of Campbell has lent
a classic charm to the beautiful scenery of the valley,
and under the title of "Gertrude of Wyoming" given
a picture of some of those earlier events that con-
verted this terrestrial paradise into a frightful waste.

When the trial was over, Dr. Johnson went from
Trenton to Philadelphia, where he was very favorably
received by Governor Dickinson and several of the
most respectable lawyers and gentlemen of that city.
It was a time for great men to confer together on the
concerns of the country, and political sagacity as well
as political knowledge and experience were brought
into requisition as opportunity offered.

Notwithstanding his course of neutrality during
the war, and the attempts which were made to cast
suspicion upon his patriotism, Connecticut, after the
cessation of hostilities, had no man of more states-
manlike views, or in whom she reposed higher confidence as a national legislator, than WILLIAM SAMUEL
JOHNSON. From November 8, 1784, to May 8, 1787,
he was in the service of the State as a delegate in
Congress, — being absent from home in this period
793 days, at 18 shillings a day, and charging to his
constituency in addition the hire of a servant for two
years and six months at thirty shillings a month.

This did not include his expenses, which formed a separate and larger item. His colleague was Stephen Mix Mitchell, of Wethersfield, who was his junior, and survived him nearly a score of years. Connecticut was poor at this time, and the services of her delegates in Congress were tardily paid, and at irregular intervals. This was occasionally embarrassing to them, as will be seen by the following letter, written to Dr. Johnson by Mr. Mitchell from Wethersfield, Sunday evening, November 13, 1785:—

Your favor of the 7th instant came safe to hand, by which I find you disappointed that so little notice was taken by the Assembly of the recommendation of Congress for sending three delegates. I urged the matter to sundry members as far as the delicacy of my situation would admit, but they had reasons which I may better communicate *vivâ voce* than by writing.

Relative to proper supplies of money, suffer me to say,—'t was not unwillingness to afford a sufficiency, but want of power to force collections any faster than by the laws enacted in May last, which prevented their doing anything on that subject. The Governor draws on the Treasurer without any particular direction from the Assembly, and there are sufficient funds provided by the civil list taxes. The fault lies at the door of the executive and legislative part of government. These taxes have long been due, yet the Treasurer informs me he cannot command a shilling to discharge your old or my new orders, but hopes the law, making the bodies of collectors liable by the first of December next, may bring in something by that day. In the mean time he bids me inform you that if any collector in your region has any cash and will deliver it you, your receipt or draught shall be passed to his credit. Our finances are in a deplorable situation, when every farthing of cash is forestalled before it reaches the Treasurer's office.

Nothing must prevent your attendance in Congress early. Could you, like good Elisha of old, impart but a single portion of your intellectual furniture to your colleagues, they might perhaps be induced by such a consideration to consent to your tarry at home for a short time. This is rather to be wished than hoped for in these days of declension. Colonel Thomas Fitch is undoubtedly in cash as naval officer, and can afford a partial supply to you. The moment I can procure a pittance, I shall come on, and am in hopes to be at New York by the time the new Congress enters upon business; although I have as yet but very faint encouragement. I am determined the officers of government shall exert themselves and procure money, and you know strong faith goes far even in temporals.

I have applied to Colonel Wadsworth, who is your friend, and told him your situation; he is a man of influence and activity; he will exert himself to supply and I believe will write you. 'Tis humiliating, indeed, to be obliged to run after a publican and ask money on such an occasion. We hope it may be otherwise anon.

Can you recommend any particular quarters to me in New York, not encumbered with company or a large family, where peace and quiet reign with easy, frugal gracefulness? If you know such will thank you for information.

A letter from New York, written by the same hand, and dated the 1st of the ensuing March, conveyed to Dr. Johnson the intelligence that his presence in Congress was indispensable. Matters had assumed an aspect threatening the unity and power of the Federal Government. The State of New Jersey, by the action of the lower house of its Assembly, had refused to comply with the requisitions of Congress issued the previous year, and had given reasons for the refusal. Members became alarmed, and, as Mr. Mitchell said in this letter, " began to look round to see who were absent, and a motion was made to send an express to Connecticut to require your attendance or that of Mr. Sturgis. After much altercation it was laid aside, and I have promised what you must perform with all possible dispatch, namely, that Connecticut should be very soon represented. Pray don't fail of adding wings to your speed. Things grow serious, and I believe we are not very distant from some great event."

He hastened to his post, and did what he could to allay the uneasiness. But the defects in the old Articles of Confederation were more and more felt as new exigencies arose. The mode of supplying the public treasury was found to be ineffectual. The delays and uncertainties incident to a revenue, to be established and collected from time to time by thirteen independent States, was not reconcilable with the punctuality essential to the proper discharge of a national obligation. The power to regulate trade and lay imposts or duties had not been thought of in framing the original act of confederation, so much as the necessity of mutual help and protection in securing the great boon of American independence. Liberty was won, and not only were the States left burdened with heavy debts, but individuals were borne down by them; and in consequence of the interruption of commerce, the scarcity of money, and the depreciation of the currency, creditors in many parts of the country went unpaid. Writs of attachment and judgments of courts became a source of irritation, and in several of the counties of Massachusetts bodies of armed men surrounded the tribunals of justice; and in New Hampshire, the Legislature was defied by a band of insurgents, which was finally dispersed by the inhabitants of the town where the session was held. The insurrection of Daniel Shays, who had been a captain in the Continental army, assumed such proportions as to call for the intervention of the State government, and a detachment of militia under General Lincoln was sent to Springfield to suppress it and to make prisoners of the lawless force.

These and other acts of insubordination elsewhere not only revealed the weakness of the General Government, but they went deep into the minds and hearts of the best statesmen of the land.

Jonathan D. Sergeant, Attorney General of Pennsylvania, writing to Johnson on the 18th of February, 1786, and asking for his favor to secure the appointment of his brother-in-law as one of the commissioners of Congress for settling accounts, gave a gloomy picture of the national prospect, when he closed his letter by saying: "What is to become of this country? I am distressed on this subject. Unless some mode is adopted for a firmer union, and vesting Congress with the power of complying with her treaties, I tremble for the consequences. I know that your people have great trust in Providence; but for my part I am so apt to connect the means with the end, that I am frightened at our neglect of the necessary steps towards our political salvation. God help us!"

It was felt that some new provision was needed to combine the power of the States, and make the enjoyment of liberty worth the price it had cost. As the Colonies did not severally act for themselves and proclaim their own independence, so they were to keep in view that the achievement of the whole was for the benefit of the whole, and would be entirely frustrated if separate and individual interests should be set up in opposition to the recommendations and demands of Congress.

Commissioners, therefore, from five of the States — New York, New Jersey, Pennsylvania, Delaware, and Virginia—met at Annapolis, Md., September 11, 1786, and conferred together on the trade and commerce of the United States, and on the regulations necessary to secure permanent harmony and the public weal. They were clothed with no powers, and being only a partial and defective representation, they ventured upon nothing beyond proposing a convention of delegates from all the States to take into consideration the situation of things, " to devise such further provisions as shall appear to them necessary to render the constitution of the Federal Government adequate to the exigencies of the Union; and to report such an act for that purpose to the United States in Congress assembled, as, when agreed to by them, and afterwards confirmed by the Legislatures of every State, will effectually provide for the same." Though these commissioners were aware that they could not with propriety address their sentiments and observations to any but those whom they had the honor to represent, yet they decided, from motives of respect, to transmit copies of their report to the Governors of other States, and to the United States in Congress assembled.

It was referred in Congress to a " Grand Committee," who embodied their views in a resolution, entirely coinciding with the commissioners as to the inefficiency of the Federal Government, and the necessity of devising some new provisions; and on the 21st day of February, 1787, the substance of the resolution was adopted in language as follows: "That in the opinion of Congress, it is expedient that on the second Monday in May next, a Convention of Delegates, who shall have been appointed by the several States, be held at Philadelphia, for the sole and express purpose of revising the Articles of Confederation, and reporting to Congress and the several Legislatures such alterations and provisions therein as shall, when agreed to in Congress, and confirmed by the States, render the Federal Constitution adequate to the exigencies of government and the preservation of the Union."

All the old Thirteen States, except Rhode Island, readily acquiesced in the proposed measure, and appointed their representatives; and the Legislature of Connecticut placed at the head of its delegation Dr. Johnson, with Roger Sherman, a signer of the Declaration of Independence, and Oliver Ellsworth, for his colleagues. A sufficient number of delegates did not appear to constitute a representation of a majority of the States until Friday, the 25th of May, when the Convention was organized and proceeded to business. Dr. Johnson was a conspicuous and influential member of that body. From the time he took his seat to the close of the session, September 17, he does not appear to have been absent from the proceedings. It is known that the deliberations were frequently impeded by jarring interests and local feelings, and his views, being wholly liberal and national, and "seeking peace in the spirit of peace," he was occasionally the happy instrument of conciliation between the fears and jealousies of the smaller States and the claims and assumptions of the larger ones. No full report of the debates in that Convention was ever made ; but Johnson himself says they " were very long, and for a long time we remained in doubt whether we should be able to effect anything; but knowing the necessity of doing something, we finally, by mutual concessions, agreed upon the present Constitution of the United States."

It is understood that the most original and peculiar feature of the government was due to his suggestion and urgency. He first proposed the organization of the Senate as a distinct body, in which the state sovereignties should be equally represented and guarded, while the weight of population might be felt in the House of Representatives. It was the morning after Dr. Franklin had made his celebrated speech in the Convention, acknowledging the difficulties which surrounded them, and closing with a proposition to seek the guidance of Divine wisdom in prayers, at the opening of each day's session, that Johnson rose in his place and said : —

As the debates have hitherto been managed, they may be spun out to an endless length ; and as gentlemen argue on different grounds, they are equally conclusive on the points they advance, but afford no demonstration either way. States are political societies. For whom are we to form a government? for the people of America, or for those societies? Undoubtedly for the latter. They must, therefore, have a voice in the second branch of the general government, if you mean to preserve their existence. The people already compose the first branch. The mixture is proper and necessary. For we cannot form a general government on any other ground.

When the Constitution had been adopted in all its parts, and printed as a whole, a committee of five was appointed by ballot " to revise the style of, and arrange the articles agreed to by the House," and Johnson was chosen the first member of this committee, with Mr. Hamilton, Mr. G. Morris, Mr. Madison, and Mr. King for his associates. The original copy, preserved in the Department of State at Washington, and a copy among the Johnson manuscripts, both contain interlineations and marginal corrections in his own handwriting, and these were embodied in the Federal Constitution, and appear in the articles as they now stand.

The instrument, as it thus came from the hands of its framers, was not considered by any one to be perfect in theory. The Thirteen States differed so widely in their situation, resources, extent, prejudices, and social interests that it was difficult to unite under a system of national government. Franklin spoke very truly, and reflected the feelings, probably, of all the delegates, when in a brief address near the close of the Convention, he said : " I consent to this Constitution, because I expect no better, and because I am not sure it is not the best. The opinions I have had of its errors, I sacrifice to the public good."

CHAPTER XI.

ELECTED PRESIDENT OF COLUMBIA COLLEGE; MEMBER OF THE
STATE CONVENTION TO ACT ON THE FEDERAL CONSTITUTION;
EPISCOPAL CHURCH AND BISHOP SEABURY; ELECTED A SENA-
TOR IN CONGRESS; JUDICIARY OF THE UNITED STATES; LET-
TERS FROM DISTINGUISHED PERSONS; REMOVAL OF CONGRESS
TO PHILADELPHIA, AND RESIGNATION AS SENATOR.

A. D. 1787–1793.

On the 21st of May, 1787, he was appointed to the
charge of Columbia College, New York, which had
fallen into decay during the war, and received but
little attention, owing to the military occupation of
the city and the suspension of regular instruction.
He thus became the first head of the Institution under
its new charter and reorganization, as his father had
been the first President under the Royal Charter, and
the old title of King's College. Mr. Duane, in communicating to him the fact of his unanimous election,
said: "The terms are the same on which we engaged that great and good man, your revered
father."

His acceptance of the office did not separate him
from the interests of his former constituents, though
it required his removal to New York. His friends
still sought his aid and counsel, for the political troubles were not yet over, and men of wisdom and expe-

9

rience were needed to give shape and support to the
best measures for establishing a federal government.
Dr. Benjamin Gale, who had been strongly opposed
to a separation of the Colonies from Great Britain, in
the manner it was effected, writing him from Killingworth on the 19th of April, 1787, said : " There will
not, nor cannot subsist harmony between the Northern and Southern States. I would as soon undertake to cement the iron and clay of Nebuchadnez-
zar's image, as to unite them cordially and sincerely.
There are but two ways by which government can
be supported in these New England States: one by
just and equitable laws judiciously executed; the
other by the sword. The latter will not, I presume,
answer in these States without the effusion of much
blood. But, Sir, permit me to tell you once more
prophetically, the hedge of government is broken
down, and never will be repaired, but it will overturn, overturn, overturn till He comes whose right
it is to reign. You must not expect it ; we are now
on the verge of Daniel's day of trouble. I look upon
this State, the backbone of this Continent. The transactions of the approaching Assembly, if judiciously
conducted, may save us ; otherwise we shall soon be
involved in blood and carnage. Come home as soon
as you can and save us from ruin."

The warmth of this appeal may have been excited
by recent tumults and disturbances in Massachusetts,
and not a little by contact with " people whose morals," to use Gale's phrase, " had been corrupted by
Authority." Repudiation of the domestic debt was
openly discussed, and the attempts of collectors to
close the arrears of taxes due to the State by " levy-

ing their executions" only tended to greater uneasiness and distress. Inability, more perhaps than a want of inclination, stood in the way of complying with the demands of the officers. "The truth I take it is," said Dr. Gale, "there is not hard money enough by one half in the State to discharge the arrears of taxes now due." The worst consequences were apprehended by the people in view of this condition of things, and the great problem to be solved was, how to avoid them, and maintain the public honor and independence.

When the Convention of Delegates from the several towns in Connecticut met by authority of the General Assembly to act on the question of accepting the Federal Constitution, Johnson was there as one of the representatives from Stratford, having left his post in College to fulfill a duty to his townsmen and native State. His two colleagues in the Federal Convention were there also, and Mr. Ellsworth, whose name was not affixed to the Constitution at Philadelphia, having left probably before the session closed, made perhaps the ablest and most elaborate speech in the State Convention in favor of its ratification.

By the 2d of July, 1788, a sufficient number of ratifications had been returned to Congress, then sitting in New York, to enable that body to examine them, and report an act for putting the Constitution into operation. Johnson was not so absorbed with his duties in the halls of Columbia, as to be indifferent to the debate on this subject, which was continued at intervals for a period of two months. Having had much to do in framing the articles and

shaping the course of previous legislation, his judgment in regard to the final action, must have been
as valuable as it was desirable.

Sometimes he was applied to for advice in matters
outside the machinery of the national government.
His Rector at Stratford wrote him on the 13th of
August, in this same year, touching the welfare of
the Episcopal Church, and the recognition of Bishop
Seabury as a step towards Ecclesiastical union. The
letter and the answer are worth producing in this
place.

HONORED SIR, — Provided you should have a convenient
opportunity, would it not be best to make inquiry of some
of the members of Congress from Virginia, whether Dr.
Griffith is gone to England to be consecrated Bishop for
that State? If he is not, and those members of Congress
should propose that Bishop Seabury be joined with the other
two Bishops, and consecrate him in America, I doubt not the
measure would be adopted. And in case it should, this good
effect would ensue, a union of the Church. As there is a
federal union of the States, it appears to me there ought
to be a union of the Church. And provided they consider
it only in a political view, will it not be the wisest method
they can pursue to insure a stability in government? And
is there any upon whom they can depend more, in a day of
trial, than those that have been tried? And is not this a
proper time for this business to be done?

I do not mean this should be a Congressional resolve, but
that these gentlemen might advise their friends to adopt the
measure, as it would save the expense, which Dr. Griffith is
not able to bear. Bishop Seabury will not make any objection, but will be ready to join the others, — which will show
where the fault is in case any objection should be made to
the measure. For reasons that I shall omit to mention, perhaps Philadelphia may be the most proper place for the Bishops to meet, in case this scheme should take place.

A union of the Church I most ardently wish, and if something is not done soon to accomplish it, I fear it will never be done.

However, after all, the propriety of your acting in the affair must be left to your better judgment to determine. The kindness you have always extended to the Church is acknowledged with the most sincere gratitude by your Honor's most obedient humble servant,

JEREMIAH LEAMING.

In reply to these suggestions, Dr. Johnson wrote : —

REV. SIR, — I inclose you a letter to Mr. Ogden in answer to the one you forwarded me from him. I will, if I have a proper opportunity, speak to the Virginia Delegates upon the subject you mention, but I much fear whether any of those who at present represent that State would give much attention to any business of that nature ; and you are sensible the two Bishops [White and Provoost] would at present give no countenance to the idea, as they conceive they are pledged to the English Bishops, that Dr. Griffith should come to them for consecration. I very sincerely join with you in ardently wishing for a union of the Church, and will omit nothing in my power to effect it, but fear it cannot be very speedily accomplished, owing to the circumstance I have mentioned, as well as others which you are not unacquainted with.

The first action of the Legislature of Connecticut, under the new Federal Constitution, was the election of Dr. Johnson as a Senator in Congress, and Oliver Ellsworth was next chosen to be his colleague. Notwithstanding his situation as President of Columbia College, he accepted the appointment, and was able to fulfill the duties of both offices without detriment to either, since this first Congress under the Federal Constitution, like previous ones, was held in the city of New York.

The business of the session was not entered upon with much dispatch, and in some quarters there was disappointment at the delay. His old friend Stephen M. Mitchell, of Wethersfield, wrote him March 22, 1789, and said : " The good people in this region are impatient with the tardiness of the new government, and conjecture there must be a defection in the friends of it. Why are the chariot wheels from the South so slow ? The opposers begin to think it will drag heavily, and they hope it will never acquire motion." It was a novel thing for Congress to sit and deliberate in separate houses, and there was a little awkwardness in beginning business in this way.

Johnson had seen during his long residence in England, the workings of the two houses of Parliament, and was among the best qualified members of the Senate. He was more than a mere ornament in that chamber of great and dignified councilors. It is not too much to say of him that he was *primus inter pares*, and contributed largely to shape those institutions, and lay down those rules which were to give to the new government its energy and direction. Among other acts of vast public importance, the bill for organizing the Judiciary of the United States was drawn up by him in concert with his colleague. This was a work that involved much labor and no little skill ; for it was necessary to establish a system which might not only promote the great ends of public justice, but, at the same time, preserve a uniformity in the mode of its administration, and maintain the authority of the national government, without encroaching upon the rights and jurisdiction of States, or rudely innovating upon their cherished forms of practice.

As a public man, he was frequently the recipient of communications from distinguished persons who had views of their own to further, or who wished to obtain his opinion on matters which, in the infancy of the government, were not well settled or very clearly defined. Sometimes the questions submitted to him were of a literary and philological character. Dr. Stiles, then President of Yale College, wrote him on the 13th of April, 1789, a full letter touching the new state of things, and pointing out what appeared to his mind objectionable features in the Constitution. The letter is too long to quote, but an extract must not be withholden in this connection. After speaking of what he conceived to be minor defects, he went on to indulge in free reveries and prophecies, which sound rather strangely in our ears at this late day.

" We shall do well upon the present Federal Constitution. Perhaps some things might be amended. But if none but the trifles I have mentioned above were found expedient to amend, I look upon them of so little importance that I should pray God they might never be amended. But there are probably others of some moment and magnitude, and worthy to be amended hereafter. But I wish to have no amendments made these twenty years; or not until by experience and good judgment we should be able to discern what amendments are necessary. The Constitution is so good and excellent, that I do not wish to have it shaken by any speedy alterations. However desirous a number of States may be for a speedy convention and revision, I wish it may be evaded and put off until we are, as a public, able to judge upon experiment. I presume the public administration by the Federal Congress will be, in its initial operations, mild, gentle, clear in its reasons; but firm and steady, and of a growing weight. And I further presume without a doubt that the more the new federal system or police is contemplated, the more diffused will be the public conviction and satisfaction, that LIBERTY is secure under it; and that it will require more ages than from this to the Millennium to advance any growing corruption into the maturity of Despotism, especially in these enlightened ages. It required seven hundred years to change the Roman Republic into an Imperial Policy, when the Policy commenced on the small territory of, say sixteen miles square, — for to the Punic Wars the Roman Dominion scarcely reached the sixteenth stone from the city; whereas our Republican Policy begins on the broad basis of a territory from the Atlantic to the Mississippi. In the initial formation of our Polity are sown largely such seeds of Republicanism, or of a *representative* and *elective patrician government*, that the intrigues of mortals had as good attempt to pluck a constellation from the firmament, as to enterprise or expect a mutation of our Polity into Despotism, arbitrary Power, or even limited Monarchy. The Millennium will find us a Republic.

A letter of quite a different character was written to him in the succeeding month by Silas Deane, the gentleman who had taken his place in the first Continental Congress, when he himself had been called away to another duty. Mr. Deane was the first diplomatic agent to France, and his contracts and engagements while abroad were such as to embarrass Congress and lead to his recall. He was suspected of misapplying the public funds intrusted to his care, and failing to dispel the suspicions and regain his reputation, he published in 1784 an address to the country asserting his integrity, and afterwards went over to England. The letter which follows was written to interest Dr. Johnson in his behalf, and it shows how great were his sorrow and destitution at the time.

LONDON, *June* 29, 1789.

SIR, — I was flattered some months since that I should have had the pleasure of seeing you in London before this, and of giving you personally the history of my past and of my present situation, hoping that I should be able thereby to convince you of the extreme injustice which I have suffered, and to interest you, from your well-known principles of justice and humanity, in my favor. In this I am disappointed by your being called on to act a more important part in the great council of the American States. Though disappointed in those expectations, I am led to form much greater on this event, and such as are not confined to the personal interest of so unimportant an individual as myself, but extending to my country at large.

In my letters to Colonel Wadsworth and to my brother, which will accompany this, I have stated my situation, and the grounds for what I now solicit so fully, that I will not trouble you with a repetition of any part in this, having requested of them to make you acquainted with the substance of my letters on this subject.

It is now almost ten years since I have solicited for an impartial inquiry into my conduct whilst in the service of my country, and for a settlement of my accounts, that justice might be done to my fortune as well as to my character ; unfortunately I have hitherto been unsuccessful. You can sufficiently imagine, without my attempting to describe, what I must have suffered on every account, during so long a period of anxiety and distress. I hope that is now drawing to a close. I have at no time solicited for favor or indulgence from the late Congress, but for justice. And it is all I ask at present. If I have in any instance betrayed, or been unfaithful in the trust reposed in me by my country, let it be made to appear. Justice to the public calls for it as well as justice to an individual. And I once more present my case before the tribunal of my country for a fair and full examination. I have been so long habituated to poverty that I can bear it, however reluctantly, but injustice to my character is insupportable.

I will trespass no further on your time, but refer you to my friends above named, and am with the most perfect respect, Sir, your most obedient and very humble servant,

S. Deane.[1]

Dr. Johnson found the claims of the Institution, over which he presided, pressing upon his attention, and prolonged absence from his post was irreconcilable with these claims. He attended the first session of Congress after its removal to Philadelphia; and then resigned his seat that he might devote himself exclusively to his collegiate duties. No man ever laid down senatorial honors more gracefully; and Governor Huntington, in acknowledging, March 22, 1793, his letter of resignation, said: "I am sorry that Connecticut and the Union should be deprived of so able a councilor in that honorable body; but must believe that in due deliberation you have discovered reasons sufficient to justify the measure you have adopted; and am satisfied that you will not fail, as opportunities shall offer, to promote the happiness and prosperity of this State."

[1] He died suddenly, shortly after the date of this letter, on board the *Boston Packet*, in the Downs. "In 1842 his long-disputed claims were adjusted by Congress, and a large sum was found to be due to his heirs, under the principles recognized by the government, and applicable to all claimants : hence the doubt whether he received entire justice at the hands of his associates. A man driven to despair is to be judged mercifully."— Sabine's *Loyalists of the American Revolution*, vol. i. p. 362.

CHAPTER XII.

TREATY WITH GREAT BRITAIN; RESPONSIBILITY AS AN EDUCA-
TOR; ADDRESS TO THE GRADUATING CLASS OF COLUMBIA COL-
LEGE; AND TIMELY COUNSELS.

A. D. 1793–1795.

DR. JOHNSON had seen enough in his intercourse
with public men to feel the importance of the high
position which he held, and to which it was now his
purpose to devote himself for the remainder of his
days. Things were not well settled in the country;
and the government, which was new to the people,
was opposed in some of its acts with an acrimony that
was due as much to ignorance of their true nature
and design as to the influence of party spirit. The
authority of the laws and the stability of the union
were threatened by insurrectionary movements; and
the ratification by the Senate of the United States of
the commercial treaty with Great Britain at a time
when that kingdom was waging war with France,
occasioned a popular excitement which was widely
spread and not easily allayed.

Judge Iredell, of North Carolina, then in Philadelphia, writing to Johnson on the 17th of August,
1795, and referring to the tendencies of education,
said: " The present period very forcibly evinces the
justice of your remark ' that science is the truest

security of liberty,' for if so great a body of ignorance as has been produced against the Treaty should
be *in constant requisition* against every other act of
government, we should soon have no government or
Liberty left. It is lamentable to see the precipitancy,
folly, and indecency with which so many rush into
the condemnation of a measure which requires the
most accurate attention, close investigation, and full
information on a great many combined considerations
upon which its merit or demerit must ultimately depend. I wish the dignity of the President's answer
may calm the emotions of those who run after the
cry of ' liberty ' and ' constitution,' without knowing
what either means, and when they are at the same
instant in the direct train to the most effectual measures to destroy both."

The reference in this extract was to the answer
which President Washington had returned to resolutions and addresses adopted in public meetings con-
demnatory of the treaty. The first resolves of this
sort proceeded from an assembly in Boston, and were
dispatched to him, with a letter from the selectmen of
the town. They were intended to affect the popular
mind and to operate on the executive, and the sup-
porters not only of the administration but of good
order had much to do in stemming the torrent of
abuse and diverting it from its course.

Johnson had a high sense of his responsibilities as
an educator at that interesting period of American
history. If his most intimate friends and political
associates entrusted to him their sons, they felt that
they were safe under his care. His brief addresses to
the graduating classes on commencement days, — a

few of which have been preserved, — show the drift
of his anxieties and the purity and strength of his
principles. It may be worth while to produce one
here, which has been found among his papers fully
written out, by way of comparing it with similar
addresses in these days. The thoughts, as expressed,
indicate a remembrance of the critical scenes through
which he had just passed in the formation of the government, and a desire that young men should not forget how they had double duties to perform in life —
duties to their Creator and to their country. But let
the address speak for itself.

The length and number of your exercises have so far ex-
hausted the time allotted us as to forbid my detaining this
very respectable audience with so detailed a charge as hath
been usual upon these occasions ; and from the specimens
you have given of your own improvement and qualifications,
I trust it will be thought quite unnecessary. I shall therefore only, in very few words, remind you of a principle which
you have been well instructed in, — that all the duties in-
cumbent upon us in life result immediately and necessarily
from the situations and relations in which we are placed, and
are therefore all founded in Reason and Truth. This is a
principle of very great importance, utility, and extent in
directing our conduct. Let me then intreat you upon all
occasions to consider well your own situations and relations,
and always to endeavor to conduct according to them ; if you
do this you will seldom err.

You this day, gentlemen, assume new characters, enter
into new relations, and consequently incur new duties. You
have, by the favor of Providence and the attention of friends,
received a public education, the purpose whereof hath been
to qualify you the better to serve your Creator and your
country. You have this day invited this audience to witness

the progress you have made, the literary honors conferred upon you, and the qualifications with which you are dismissed to take your stations in society. You have then here pledged yourselves in the presence of this assembly that you are worthy of the liberal education you have received, and of the honors conferred upon you. Thus you assume the character of scholars, of men, and of citizens, great and important characters demanding various and exalted duties. Go, then, gentlemen, and exercise them with diligence, fidelity, and zeal. Fulfill the expectations your friends have a right to form of you, and the demands which your country hath upon you.

Your first great duties, you are sensible, are those you owe to Heaven, to your Creator and Redeemer. Let these be ever present to your minds, and exemplified in your lives and conduct. Imprint deep upon your minds the principles of piety towards God, and a reverence and fear of His holy name. The fear of God is the beginning of wisdom and its consummation is everlasting felicity. Possess yourselves of just and elevated notions of the Divine character, attributes, and administration, and of the end and dignity of your own immortal nature as it stands related to Him. Reflect deeply and often upon those relations. Remember that it is in God you live and move and have your being, — that in the language of David He is about your bed and about your path and spieth out all your ways, — that there is not a thought in your hearts, nor a word upon your tongues, but lo! he knoweth them altogether, and that he will one day call you to a strict account for all your conduct in this mortal life. Remember, too, that you are the redeemed of the Lord, that you are bought with a price, even the inestimable price of the precious blood of the Son of God. Adore Jehovah, therefore, as your God and your Judge. Love, fear, and serve Him as your Creator, Redeemer, and Sanctifier. Acquaint yourselves with Him in His word and holy ordinances. Make Him your friend and protector and your felicity is secured both here and hereafter. And with respect to particular duties to Him, it is your happiness that you are well assured that he best serves his Maker, who does most good to his country and to mankind.

As scholars, it is your duty, continually to cultivate your minds and improve in every branch of useful science. Remember that your minds are properly yourselves, — your better part which is to continue and act in a more exalted state of existence, when you shall have done with time and sense. How infinitely important then is it that you form them to wisdom and virtue. In this seminary, you have only entered the portals of the Temple of Science. You have yet to survey and examine the august building in all its dimensions and extent, in all its grand and spacious apartments with all their various uses and ornaments. Here you could only lay the foundations of science, the superstructure . is yet to be reared, but they are such foundations as I trust you may build upon to great advantage so as to render you happy in yourselves and useful to society. I say useful to society — for remember always that whatever internal pleasure, external splendor, or personal emolument of any kind you may derive from the cultivation of science, you are not to rest here. All knowledge is designed for use, and not for our own use only, but for the benefit of others also. We are born, says Cicero, very justly, not for ourselves only, but partly for our friends and partly for our country ; and give me leave to add with Cato, in part also for all mankind. For to relieve the oppressed and to do good to all men, is the most glorious art that man is capable of, and that which gives him the nearest possible resemblance to his divine Maker. It is also attended with the sublimest pleasure the human heart can feel, — a heavenly pleasure, known only to those who are of a truly beneficent, enlarged, and benevolent disposition. As men, then, and in all your commerce with mankind, you must be just and upright, true and faithful, kind and merciful, affable and benevolent : be useful upon all occasions to the utmost of your abilities, and apply all the knowledge you have acquired or shall acquire to the benefit of mankind, endeavoring always to render them wiser and better.

As citizens, you are under every obligation, human and divine, to exert every faculty that God has blessed you with, and to embrace every opportunity that He may furnish you with, to promote, as far as possible, the peace, prosperity, and happiness of your country, and to devote all your talents and acquisitions, and even life itself, if need be, to its service: to awaken continually in your own bosoms, and to diffuse, as far as possible, around you every principle of public virtue and love of country that they may be drawn forth into action, to effectuate and accomplish that great and glorious and godlike design, the general happiness of civil society and the universal felicity of all mankind.

Such, gentlemen, are the obligations you are under. These are the duties which you have this day in this respectable presence pledged yourselves to perform as far as a gracious Providence shall enable you and give you opportunity to discharge them. This is an ample field for the display of all your talents and all your virtues. Cultivate it, I beseech you, diligently. Your own honor and reputation in life demand it of you. The reputation and honor of this seminary of learning, your Alma Mater, in which you have been so long and so tenderly nursed, the glory, the prosperity, and happiness of your country, that dear country which hath not only given you birth, but an honorable birthright and title to all the distinguishing privileges of freemen, all, I say, with united voices demand of you a diligent attention to the discharge of those important and honorable duties. Let them not demand in vain. Study carefully the fundamental principles of civil government, especially of Republican Government. Make yourselves well acquainted with the true nature of civil liberty, which, fond as we all justly are of it, too many seem to be unacquainted with. Study the true industry of your country. See what will render it happy at home and respectable abroad. Examine its present situation and what will be the effect of union, order, harmony, a firm government of laws and an energetic execution of them. See whether true Liberty does not consist in an exact obedience to law, a submission to the public will, a surrender of all individual, inferior, partial, subordinate interests, emoluments, and objects to general, public, and universal welfare.

Desert not then the station you have assumed, the post which Providence hath assigned you, — but go forth into the world firmly resolved neither to be allured by its vanities nor contaminated by its vices, but to run with patience and perseverance, with firmness and alacrity, the glorious career of Religion, honor, and virtue. I say again, the glorious career of Religion, honor, and virtue, for in this career alone, be assured, is true glory to be acquired, real glory and honor in this life, and everlasting glory and felicity in the life to come. Finally, gentlemen, in the elegant and expressive language of St. Paul, "Whatsoever things are *true*, whatsoever things are *honest*, whatsoever things are *just*, whatsoever things are *pure*, whatsoever things are *lovely*, whatsoever things are of *good report*, if there be any virtue, and if there be any praise, think on these things" and do them, and the God of peace shall be with you, to whose most gracious protection I now commend you, humbly imploring Almighty Goodness that He will be your guardian and your guide, your protector and the rock of your defence, your Saviour and your God.

These were not the sentiments and utterances of a Christian divine, but of a layman, a Christian statesman, whose varied experience and knowledge of the world gave weight to his counsels and wisdom to his exhortations. They were alike worthy of his head and of his heart, and showed what a lustre Christian learning can shed over talents and over station. The young men in those days who listened to them and held them in remembrance, must have been inspired

10

with a high sense of their personal responsibility as the creatures of God and beings entrusted with a revelation.

Parents and guardians could not refrain from expressing their gratitude for his care and attention, or as one of them turned the thought, — " for the troublesome duty you have imposed on yourself in forming the mind of your young pupil, and fitting him for the part he may hereafter have to perform in life." Thus he did not believe in any high intellectual culture separate from the spirit of sound morality and the principles of the Christian faith. A complete education, whether it related to the training of the character or of the intellect, involved, in his view, the use of religious motives and influences. For society being composed of individuals must depend for its welfare and advancement on the aggregate sentiments of its constituent members, and therefore he would have no young man, who came under his oversight and tuition, shut from his mind the idea of God and moral accountability.

His counsels, as given in the foregoing address, were timely. If the political state of things in his own country made them pertinent, they were needed far more in view of that gigantic madness which was yet prevailing in France, and sapping and undermining the very foundations of social order and true morality. Dr. Dwight, who was elected to the Presidency of Yale College in 1795, delivered a discourse five years after his election, " on some events in the last century," in which he took occasion to speak of the influence of the leaders in the late French Revolution, and of the strong sympathy manifested in this country with their principles and declarations. "They were viewed," said he, "merely as human beings, embarked deeply in the glorious cause of liberty, and not at all as infidels, as the abettors of falsehood, and the enemies of righteousness, of truth, and of God. Hence all their concerns were felt, and all their conduct covered with the veil of charity. They were viewed as having adventured and suffered together with ourselves, and as now enlisted for the support of a kindred cause. The consequences of these prejudices were such as would naturally be expected. A general and unexampled confidence was soon felt, and manifested by every licentious man. Every infidel, particularly, claimed a new importance, and treated religion with enhanced contempt. The graver ones, indeed, through an affected tenderness for the votaries of Christianity, adopted a more decent manner of despising it ; but all were secure of a triumph, and satisfied that talents, character, and the great world were on their side. The young, the ardent, the ambitious, the voluptuous were irresistibly solicited to join a cause which harmonized with all their corruptions ; pointed out the certain road to reputation, and administered the necessary opiates to conscience ; and could not refuse to unite themselves with men, who spoke great swelling words of vanity, who allured them through much wantonness, and promised them the unbounded liberty of indulging every propensity to pleasure. The timid at the same time were terrified, the orderly let loose, the sober amazed, and the religious shocked beyond example ; while the floating part of our countrymen, accustomed to swim with every tide, moved onward in obedience to the impulse. Thus principles were yielded, useful habits relaxed, and a new degree of irreligion extensively prevailed."

Such a period in national history called especially upon men at the head of educational institutions to speak with no " uncertain sound," and Johnson was one who did not hesitate to join with others, sagacious and far seeing, in commending to the youth of the land " the glorious career of religion, honor, and virtue."

CHAPTER XIII.

PROPOSITION TO PUBLISH HIS LETTERS WHILE COLONIAL AGENT;
COLUMBIA COLLEGE AND LEGISLATIVE AID; CORRESPONDENCE
WITH FRIENDS; PORTRAIT BY GILBERT STUART; HEBREW
POINTS; RESIGNATION OF THE PRESIDENCY; AND RETIREMENT
TO STRATFORD.

A. D. 1795–1800.

TOWARDS the end of the year 1795 the anxieties
of Dr. Johnson became very much excited by a proposition from Dr. Jeremiah Belknap, Corresponding
Secretary of the Massachusetts Historical Society, to
publish in its collections a volume of his letters to
the Chief Magistrate of Connecticut, written during
his agency in England from 1767 to 1771. It appears that the papers of the Trumbull family had
been allowed by its members, ostensibly for safe keeping, to pass out of their hands, and coming into the
possession of Dr. Belknap, he found these letters full
of interest and of great value, and was ready to send
them at once to the press, not however till his sense
of delicacy had led him to consult their author. Dr.
Johnson made a strenuous and somewhat indignant
remonstrance against this proceeding. It stirred in
him feelings of the utmost displeasure. He admitted
that while agent of the Colony of Connecticut he had
written many letters to Governor Pitkin and Gov-

ernor Trumbull, some of them of a private and others
of a public nature addressed to the General Assembly.
Neither class could rightfully become the property of
any Society, however respectable it might be.   His
private letters by the laws of friendship were sacred
in the hands of the family, and could not be delivered
to anybody but himself; and those of a public character, after having been communicated to the General
Assembly should have been deposited in the archives
of the State according to legislative usage.   He felt
that, if he consented to the printing, he would not
only be guilty of a breach of public trust, but of an
"atrocious injury" to the memory of Governor Trumbull and his family.   He could have had no solicitude
about his own good name in the matter.   The publication would have done him honor, as he appears in
the letters to have been a firm friend to the liberties
of his country, and a faithful, vigilant, discerning
agent, detecting the artifices, evasions, and blunders of
the British ministry, and giving the best information,
advice, and caution to his employers.   But the scheme
of printing was abandoned, and Dr. Belknap paid him
a high compliment as he relinquished it, by saying:
" I have read the letters repeatedly with delight, and
have gained a better idea of the political system than
from all the books published during that period."

The College drew its students principally from
New York, and its reputation was best understood
within the limits of the city.   The effort to make it
more known to the public and to obtain for it some
legislative aid are indicated by the following letter
from one of the Faculty of Medicine, dated,

ALBANY, *February* 29, 1796.

SIR, — It has a number of times occurred to me that I ought to have written to you before, and I now beg your excuse for having neglected it so long. To you who know so well what kind of life a member of Legislature must lead, it will be unnecessary to tell that in studying the order of the day, serving on committees, preparing and debating bills, resolutions, and motions, and in enlarging one's circle of acquaintance, almost all my time has been employed.

I wished for an opportunity to draw something forth from the public purse for the benefit of our College, and watched the introduction of the Treasurer's Abstract and Comptroller's Report on the state of our Finances. To my great sorrow it appeared that our income was already entirely absorbed by existing appropriations, and that the Government was actually in debt for a very large amount to the Bank of New York, which remains at this moment unpaid. The fund whence the Treasury is intended to be recruited is to be drawn from the quit-rents, and a Bill has passed both houses for that purpose; but what substantial supply will this be, when the people are allowed to pay up their arrearages and make commutation in stock of the United States? The prospects of getting something allowed to the Medical Professors all vanished immediately of course, and the labors of those meritorious and public spirited gentlemen remain to be compensated by the inconsiderable fees of tuition. The getting anything for completing the *New Building* seems utterly out of the question. But notwithstanding all this I have neither been silent nor idle. I have talked with the Chancellor of the University, and I was much concerned to find him blame in several instances, the conduct of the Trustees, in the leases and bargains made of their lands. I gave him a copy of the Report of the Faculty of Physick to be laid before the Regents. I have talked with Mr. Ellison, one of the committee to make the annual Report to the Legislature, and have had from him a sketch of what is intended. I find the President of Union College in a violent dispute with the before-named Regent about the classical learning of the President, which has been denied by the Regent, and the President seems so little satisfied with Schenectady, that were it not for the sake of his health, it is said he would return to his former place of residence and dwell among his parishioners. The academies are dwindling fast to common schools. But I need not dwell much on the Regent's Report; it will soon be before the Legislature and the public will get it through the newspapers. These reports however are at best, you know, of little consequence, as they have very trifling effect upon either the Legislature or the public.

In the debate on the *Practice of Physick Bill*, I took an opportunity to pronounce an eulogium on Columbia College to the Assembly. And in the annual *address to the Agricultural Society* which, by appointment, I delivered and to a very crowded audience in the City Hall of Albany, I introduced our seminary to the best advantage I could once more. It is surprising how little is known about Columbia College, among the citizens of this State! I have spoken fair and kind words, and given Alma Mater a goodly name.

I inclose you a printed Bill or two. That concerning the Clergymen's Corporation may be gratifying to Dr. Beach; the other concerning Aliens, has been negatived in the Assembly, though now renewed in the Senate.

Mr. Wetmore, the missionary, wrote me a few days ago that he had solicited the degree of A. M. He appears to me a well disposed and worthy young man, and I wish he could be accommodated. As to Science, a few days ago, I examined here Mr. Lent, our student's dissertation, and put a perlegi to it. I have just received a very polite letter from Dr. Priestley, relative to my proposed accommodation between the chemists. And Professor Woodhouse's new publication with a note from the author has just now come into my hands. The meetings of the Agricultural Society are numerous, frequent, and agreeable. Several valuable communications have been made. The Oneida Indians are in town and I am appointed one of a committee to confer with

them about the sale of a part of their reservation. Please
to make my compliments to Mrs. Kneeland and to my colleagues, Kemp and Wilson.

With high respect and attachment I am very unfeignedly,
yours.   SAM. L. MITCHILL.

To DR. JOHNSON.

On Sunday the 24th of April, 1796, his wife, whose
health had been declining for several months, died in
New York, and two days thereafter he sailed with her
remains in a packet for Stratford, where they were
interred in the family vault. It was but a week pre-
ceding the annual Commencement, and he was obliged
at once to return and resume his duties in college.

As might be expected, the correspondence with old
friends occasionally reverted to the troubles and trials
through which they had passed and brought to remembrance painful things. His residence in New
York and his position as the head of the college, de-
manded of him a free exercise of the rites of hospi-
tality, and his house was like a paternal home to
young men who approached him for kind offices.

Edward Rutledge of South Carolina, a signer of the
Declaration of Independence, in asking him to undertake the charge of his son, referred to his known acts
of benevolence, and said, " you certainly must delight
in them if you consent to take under your immediate
protection a youth in a strange country, and point
out to him the road to happiness through the paths
of virtue and wisdom."

His father's friend, Dr. Charles Inglis, Bishop of
Nova Scotia, a fearless and conscientious loyalist, who,
at the close of the Revolution, resigned the Rector-

ship of Trinity Church, and retired to the British
Provinces, sent his son in the beginning of the summer of 1796, on a visit to his surviving relatives in
New York, his native city, preparatory to his embark-
ing for England, where he was to finish his education.
In the letter of introduction to Dr. Johnson, that follows, there is a tone of sadness which was evidently
deepened by the Reign of Terror in France, a nation
at that time convulsed by civil war and fighting
single-handed against the greater part of Europe.

CLERMONT in Nova Scotia, June 13, 1796.

SIR, — The bearer of this is my son, whom I beg leave to
introduce to you. For some years past he has been at the
seminary which was founded in this Province soon after my
arrival; and as soon as the present horrid war is ended, I
propose to send him to England to finish his education at
Oxford.

Previous to his embarkation he visits his native city, and
his surviving relatives there; and it is my wish that he
should take a view of the college over which you, by a kind
of hereditary succession, so worthily preside, and in whose
prosperity I once felt myself deeply interested. Indeed, I
still wish it success; and hope that under your direction it
will be subservient to the purposes for which it was originally intended — the promoting sound religion and useful
literature.

Many strange revolutions and events have taken place in
Europe and America since I had the pleasure of seeing you.
To a reflecting mind, they present objects no less awful than
new and instructing. Man can see but a little way into fu-
turity, and even of those objects and events that pass before
him, he scarcely penetrates beyond the surface without comprehending their design or connection with the past and the
future. One thing we are sure of, that the affairs of this

world are under the direction of a wise and steady Providence; that the disorders which prevail for a time will be
overruled, and contribute, however unconscious the actors
may be of it, to accomplish the divine purpose. Times like
the present are clearly predicted in sacred writ, and although
the occurrences which have happened within our memory
have been such as baffled all human calculation, they may
be no more than preludes to occurrences still more surprising, and farther removed from the deductions of our limited
faculties.

   In this general expectation I conceive we are warranted
by Holy Scripture, soberly and rationally interpreted. But
when men presume to substitute fanciful conjectures for such
interpretations, and to commence prophets by pointing out
particular events, assigning with precision the time and
manner of their coming to pass; no wonder that they fall
into errors and absurd reveries; and thereby reflect discredit
on the oracles of truth.

   Our new college is erected but not quite finished. It is an
elegant structure, somewhat larger than the college of New
York; but like all buildings in this Province, which is still
in its infancy, it is of wood. The war has hitherto prevented
the full execution of our plan, and the passing our Charter,
a draft of which was drawn up [by] the King's Attorney
General four years ago. Parliament has granted £4,500
sterling to erect the edifice, and we expect His Majesty will
endow the Institution with salaries for a President and three
Professors, and also with some scholarships. The Legislature of this Province has contributed liberally to the Institution. Should it please God to restore peace, I flatter myself
that King's College at Windsor will soon be in a flourishing
state.

   What changes have taken place in your family since I last
saw you, I know not. Doubtless there have been some; but
my remote situation, and the confusions of the times pre-
cluded me from the knowledge of them. My family consists

of two daughters, grown up, and a son, the bearer of this letter.

    Sincerely wishing you happiness,

        I have the honor to be, Sir,

            your most obedient

                and humble servant.

                    CHARLES, NOVA SCOTIA.

DR. JOHNSON.

His portrait in the scarlet robe of an Oxford Doctor of Civil Law was one of the first pictures painted by Gilbert Stuart after the return of that celebrated artist to this country in 1793. Copies of it by less distinguished painters adorn the walls of Yale and Trinity Colleges, Connecticut; and Columbia possesses a very fine portrait of him in the same style and dress. There is a curious history connected with the original painting by Stuart. Dunlap, in the first volume of his "History of the Rise and Progress of the Arts of Design in the United States," says it was borrowed of Dr. Johnson's son by a Frenchman, for the purpose of study, and after it had been retained for a long time, "a copy was at length returned which deceived the owner, and the swindler kept the original." Besides stating the thing rather harshly, this is a poor compliment to the critical discernment of Mr. Johnson, and is not in accordance with the facts as contained in the following letter : —

    SIR, — I am happy, very *happy* in having it in my power to restore so valuable a picture to your possession as that of your portrait, painted by Stuart. It will be necessary for me to account to you how it came into my possession. Thus then, sir, at the time that a Mr. Graham got the picture from you, he lived with me, but a very short time after left my house and moved to Maiden Lane, and some time after left this city entirely for Philadelphia. This last removal was in consequence of having imprudently involved himself. I do not think he actually intended a dishonesty in any of his conduct, but being of a weak mind was operated on by the immediate circumstance. I have myself been much a sufferer by his misconduct. Notwithstanding some difference had taken place between us previous to his going from this city, I gave up my resentment in order to make inquiry concerning your portrait, which I looked upon as an irreparable loss to your family. I have written many times to Boston (to which place he went about two years agone), and learnt that the portrait was left in Philadelphia, and after much difficulty have been able to get it, — the person with whom I found (by proxy) refusing to deliver it for a long time, and until I procured an order. I am much rewarded for my trouble in the pleasure of delivering it to your possession, and am with the highest respect and esteem,

Your most obedient, humble servant.

DAVID LONGWORTH.

NEW YORK, *August* 8, 1798.

The writer of this letter was a liberal publisher and friend of the arts, and added in a postcript, " I should have informed you long since where the picture was, if I had supposed it could have been attended with possible good effects."

Dr. Johnson acknowledged its ʾreception with his most hearty thanks, and said, " The picture belonged to my son[1] who is now in London, and I imagine he had given up all hope of seeing it again, but I am sure will be much pleased and hold himself extremely

---

[1] Robert Charles Johnson. The original picture is now in possession of his son, Mr. Charles F. Johnson of Owego, New York, and the copy sent home by Graham as the original is in the possession of Mr. William Samuel Johnson of Stratford.

obliged to you for recovering it for him. It is a singular service that you have done us."

The prominence of his position and the interest that he took in ecclesiastical matters led to inquiries which he never failed to answer with becoming modesty. Among those who frequently consulted him was the Rev. William Smith, D. D., a Scotsman, who possessed singular versatility of talents and figured largely in the history of the Episcopal Church in Connecticut at that period. The following correspondence, though occupied mainly with the Hebrew points, touches upon a theological controversy which had grown out of the recent sermon delivered by Dr. Smith at the consecration of Bishop Jarvis.

SIR, — Long before now I expected to have had the pleasure of presenting you with a copy of my reply to Mr. Blatchford, but the printer and book-binder have been so blundering and dilatory, that, though I desired to have some copies full bound for the purpose of presenting to my friends, I have not been able to obtain any but such as I beg leave to ask your acceptance of, which I hope you will be pleased to regard, not for the merit of the author, but as a token of his respect, and for the importance of the subject.

Soon after the publicity of my reply, the Connecticut newspapers attacked me from all quarters. Of these squibs I took as little notice as was compatible with present safety, and in the meantime wrote, as a general answer, a short work entitled "An Epistle to the Co-partnership of the Rev. Mr. Blatchford." This epistle I put into the hands of Messrs. Shelton and Baldwin, who with others of the clergy approve of it, and it remains in manuscript, as a whip over these men's backs should they again come forward.

I have very much wished to have a conference with you concerning the Hebrew points, but many things at present denude me of that privilege; however you will pardon me if I hazard a conjecture concerning them; which, however, it appears to me highly probable may merit the censure of those who know much more of the sacred language than I do.

The advocates for the necessity of the points plead that they commenced, when the Hebrew language became a dead language, about the ninth or tenth century, to fix the vowel pronunciation and to distinguish words of different meaning, but of the same orthography. If this should be admitted, it will follow, that, should the English language cease at any future period to be a vivâ voce language, and only written and learned as a classical language, vowel points, similar to those presently annexed to the Hebrew character, will be deemed necessary to discriminate a number of words in our vernacular tongue, which radically differ in meaning, though subjected to the same orthography. But if the supposition, that the Masoretic points were added to the Hebrew language to supply for its paucity of real vowels, were admissible, surely a similar hypothesis were inadmissible with regard to the English language, which never complains of any want of vowels, though it seems to be burdened with too much sameness of sound in words of the same orthography but of different meaning. The more I examine the commonly received hypothesis about the Masoretic points the less of my belief they gain.

I will mention here one insurmountable objection to them, all the copies of the Pentateuch in use in the Synagogues throughout the earth have no points, and the Jews consider points as inadmissible into the service of the holy Ahhim.

.   .   .   .

Health and prosperity attend your exertions in the cause of literature and science, is the hearty wish of
Sir, your most humble servant.
WILLIAM SMITH.

NORWALK, 12th March, 1799.

To this letter Dr. Johnson replied, —

REVEREND AND DEAR SIR, — I received your favor of the 12th of March, with the very acceptable present of your answer to Mr. B., for which I return you hearty thanks. I had, by favor of Mr. Baldwin, read it soon after it was published with much pleasure and greatest satisfaction to find that we had in you so learned and able a defender of our ecclesiastical constitution. I then thought Mr. B. would never attempt to answer, and have since heard that he has declined it, in which in my opinion he has decided wisely, for it is beyond his reach, if I am not much mistaken in him, both in argument and literature.

I am obliged to you for your observations relative to the Masoretic points. They appear to me to be ingenious and probable. But I am not sufficiently acquainted with Mosaic or Hebraic literature to give a decided opinion upon so intricate a question. The Hutchinsonians have said and endeavored to prove that those points were inserted and applied by the apostate Jews to disguise and evade the prophecies relative to the Messias which were, as they said, in the original reading not plainly (for them) fulfilled in Jesus of Nazareth, in which I have in some measure acquiesced. Nor does this prove to be altogether inconsistent with your idea, as they may have answered in some measure both purposes.

I shall as I have opportunity mention your idea to our Hebrew instructor, and if anything worthy of your notice occurs, acquaint you of it. In the meantime I beg you will excuse the necessity I am under by the tremor of my hand to ask the favor of my son to assure you that I am

> Reverend and dear sir,
> Your most obedient, and
> Obliged humble servant.

In the beginning of the next year, Dr. Smith wrote him again on a kindred subject, but he was then in a feeble condition, and unable to apply his mind to matters involving much research. The letter, however, of his ingenious and learned friend has, in addition to its main object, some historical references which entitle it to a place in these pages.

DEAR SIR,—When I had the happiness of being last with you, we had some conversation about a computation of the precise day of Christmas deducible from the sacerdotal courses of the ancient Jewish Church, recorded 1 Chron. ch. 24. I now do myself the pleasure of transmitting a copy of that computation, and hope it will meet your approbation.

Another letter is put to the press, four times as long as the former, in which I calculate from the day of the dedication of Solomon's Temple, and the result comes out the same as in my calculation from the dedication of the second Temple. To evade the force of objections arising from the assertion or supposition that these courses were so interrupted either under the first or the second Temple, or during the Babylonish Captivity, that no certain computations are deducible from them, I have brought both positive and circumstantial proof that there was no chronological, though there no doubt were several executive interruptions during those periods. And if my proofs are irrefragable, the consequence is so too. Several authors are against me, and but few for me ; the Bible is for me : Ezek. c. 44, v. 15, 16 ; 1 Chron. c. 2, v. 35 ; and Ezek. c. 44, v. 8, and several others. But Scaliger and his followers are all against me. Truth is truth whoever are for or against it. " Multitudo amicorum vel inimicorum naturam veritatis non mutat." We all know that Dionysius Exiguus erred egregiously in his introducing the vulgar era, as it is called, by putting it four years later than that of Biblical chronology. Beda followed him, and a great majority of the Roman and Greek Communions did the same : and if so, why may it not be possible that Scaliger's opinion concerning the courses of the priests, may have been equally erroneous, although it has drawn almost every one into its vortex, and put a stop to all inquiry into the subject.

I have likewise sent for your perusal an Office of Induction.   It has been used both at Newtown and Ripton, with much approbation, within the course of last month and this.

Thus, sir, you see my pen is kept agoing, and if I can either be instrumental in doing good or preventing evil, I bless God for the trust put into my hands, and that His grace enables me, though but in part, to execute it.

The Church has, as she must expect to have, many enemies, and if her clergy suffer attacks to be made upon her without repelling them from what is called in popular language *catholicism*, they but unite with the adversary, instead of being faithful soldiers under Christ.

Now, a word about my going to Santa Cruz.   The people in this parish, I find, are determined to oppose the Canon of General Convention that ordains the settlement of ministers *ad vitam aut culpam*, and to hire (as they term it), their minister, from year to year.   This scheme is unknown to the Christian world, and in its consequences must prove so fatal to the Church that I scruple not to call it antichristian. 'Squire Belden is the great propagator of this opinion.   But he could never suffer the clergyman of Norwalk to rest in peace, although a pretended great friend to the Church.

Please to accept of my best wishes for your health and happiness, — and remember me as your most affectionate friend and very humble servant.

WILLIAM SMITH.

NORWALK, 27 *Jan.* 1800.

After his removal to New York, Dr. Johnson was chosen a vestryman of Trinity Church, and continued in that office till his retirement from the Presidency of the College.   Upon the death of General Washington, Dec. 14, 1799, he was summoned to attend a meeting of the corporation, called to consider what would be the best and most becoming method of solemnizing the event.   The meeting took place on a very stormy night of snow and rain, and the exposure gave him what was termed a heavy cold, which was soon followed by a severe attack of the gout. The illness confined him to his house till the succeeding spring, when despairing of recovery and wishing to die in his Stratford home and be laid by the side of his wife, he ordered himself to be carried on board a vessel and conveyed to his native village.

On the 2d of July he tendered his resignation of the Presidency, and its acceptance was couched in language as comprehensive as it is forcible. It is worthy of being quoted here in full.

NEW YORK, 21st *July*, 1800.

SIR, — The Trustees have received your letter of the 2d inst., announcing your resignation of the Presidency of Columbia College, and they have directed me to express to you their thanks for your long and faithful services in that office ; the regret they feel that the delicate state of your health prevents your continuing therein, and their wishes for your welfare *here* and happiness *hereafter*.

Though their connection with you as President of the Institution intrusted to their care will now cease, their gratitude for past services, respect for your character, and affection for your person *never will*.

By order of the Board of Trustees of Columbia College,
ABRM. BEACH, *Clerk.*

The air of his native place and relief from the anxiety of public duties became a refreshment to him, and his health, in a measure, revived. He had not yet reached his seventy-third birthday when he went into retirement, but he had done enough in all situations to demand repose, and at best his infirmities were such as to unfit him for continuance in the presidency of the college.

CHAPTER XIV.

LITERARY LEISURE; PRONUNCIATION OF GOOD SPEAKERS; VISIT
TO THE SUPERIOR COURT OF FAIRFIELD COUNTY; GENUINE
PATRIOTISM; AND LETTERS FROM HIS GRANDSON IN EUROPE.

A. D. 1800–1817.

NOTWITHSTANDING his enfeebled condition, deafness,
and a tremor in his hand, Dr. Johnson retained the
vigor and activity of his mind, the ardor of his literary
curiosity, and the most lively interest in all that concerned the welfare of his country and of the civilized
world.   His was a true enjoyment of the *otium cum
dignitate*, and younger men who visited him in his
retirement appear to have been surprised at the wealth
of his intellect and attainments.

His large library afforded him the opportunity of
keeping himself fresh in the reading of the British
classics, and as he could not well use his pen, he was
wont to pour out the stores of his knowledge to visit-
ors who sought his society, and could appreciate his
varied acquirements, and especially his familiarity with
the history of the government.   There was apparently
no attempt to make a display of knowledge.   True
learning is never ostentatious, and persons of the best
cultured minds have the least vanity.   They know
their strength for the most part, and live upon the
enjoyment of their resources.   It is stated in a paper

of the "Spectator" that "the design of learning is either to render a man an agreeable companion to himself, and teach him to support solitude with pleasure; or, if he is not born to an estate, to supply that defect, and furnish him with some means of acquiring one." Johnson, who had been flattered and courted for two generations, was in the decline of life, above the desire of seeking the notice and applause of others. So far as related to political events and transactions of which he could say *pars magna fui*, he seems to have been rather silent, for no utterances about them are on record, except where he wished to correct erroneous statements, or to give advice that might be of advantage to posterity. It has been seen how ready he was to impart information when it was solicited by friends for public or private purposes. The wonder is that so much of his correspondence, — the earlier and the later, — has escaped the common destruction to which manuscripts in the last century were doomed. A letter from Dr. Webster, author of the American Dictionary of the English Language, with its answer, will interest all who would know how the pronunciation of a single class of words has changed since he was in England, acting as the agent of the Colony of Connecticut. The letter of inquiry was dated from

NEW HAVEN, April 20, 1807.

SIR, — As you spent a few years in England in the early part of your life, I presume you must have been attentive to the pronunciation of good speakers, at the Bar, in Parliament, and on the Stage. I therefore take the liberty to inquire, sir, whether the practice of converting *u* into *yu*, or rather *t* into *ch* before *u*, as in nature, *nachure*, was prevalent at that time ; whether it was known at all — and if so, how general it was in good company. As this practice has been spreading for some years, in this country, on the authority of English books, it would gratify me to know the date of the origin of it in England ; and any facts that may throw light upon this important change in the powers of our letters. That it is not ancient is certain — nor is it deducible from any correct English principles, for our ancestors certainly had no knowledge of it. But the true origin is not well known, and any light which you can throw on the subject will be valuable to me and probably to your country.

Accept, Sir, of my high respects,

And believe me your Obed't Servant,

N. WEBSTER.

Dr. Johnson replied briefly as follows : —

" I am disabled by a paralytical affection of my hand from answering, particularly, yours of the 20th, respecting the pronunciation of the words you refer to. At the time I went to England in 1766 we pronounced the word in this country, you mention, as if it was spelt *nater ;* when I arrived in England I found it was universally pronounced nat*u*re, with the full sound of the *u*, and I heard nothing of the *ch* pronunciation until the latter part of my residence in that country, when I first heard it at the Theatre, at the time when Powell, Holland, etc., were the principal actors, after Mr. Garrick had almost retired ; and I perceived that it was adopted by some of the younger barristers and members of Parliament, but had not become common. Mr. Sheridan, who had been the preceptor of Mr. Wedderburn, and many other eminent speakers at that time, began to be considered in a great degree the standard of pronunciators. How he has determined it you will see by his Dictionary."

On the 9th of January, 1812, while the Superior Court was sitting in Fairfield, Dr. Johnson walked in and took a seat at the bar. "The presence," says a contemporary, "of this venerable and celebrated Counsellor, who has often been styled *the father of the Bar in Connecticut*, and who has probably not appeared in a Court of Justice for nearly twenty-seven years, attracted the attention of all who were present." Shortly after adjournment, the legal gentlemen in attendance held a meeting, and appointed a Committee of their number to tender him, in their behalf, a formal and written address, expressive of their interest in his personal welfare, and of their high veneration for his professional and private character, "which," said they, "has ever been considered as the brightest ornament of the Connecticut Bar." The names of Samuel B. Sherwood, Roger M. Sherman, Matthew B. Whittlesey, and James Gould, appear on the Committee, to whom Dr. Johnson, in the presence of the Judges of the Court, and other gentlemen, made a handsome verbal reply, his infirmities, especially the tremor in his hand, compelling him to adopt this mode.

Dr. Dwight said of him in 1815, he "may be considered as the representative of his contemporaries of a former age, whom time has spared for the purpose of pointing out to their children the true policy of this State. His is genuine patriotism, not bounded by the limits of any party or sect; it has survived every possible measure of ambition, and flourishes in his aged breast like the evergreen amidst the snows of ninety winters. Such patriotism may well command our respect, but it still more deserves our imitation."

A friend who had visited him at Stratford, in midsummer, 1816, and taken from him a message to President Madison, then at his seat in Virginia, received these complimentary words, which were immediately transmitted to Dr. Johnson : " It gives me pleasure to hear that Doctor Johnson enjoys, at so great an age, the blessing, so unusual, of faculties unimpaired. I have always felt a large share of the respect acknowledged by all to be due to his endowments and virtues, and, should it fall in your way, I hope you will make him sensible of the value I put on the kind expressions you have repeated from him."

Near the end of the year 1815, his grandson, the late Gulian C. Verplanck,[1] went to Charleston, and from thence to Europe, with his invalid wife, hoping, as physicians had assured him, that the voyage and a residence in the South of France, for a short time, might have the beneficial effect of restoring her to health. Among the letters which he wrote to his

[1] Daniel C. Verplanck, of Fishkill, N. Y., married October 29, 1785, *Elizabeth*, fifth daughter of William Samuel and Ann Johnson. She died February 26, 1789, in the twenty-fifth year of her age, leaving two children, GULIAN CROMMELIN, and ANN who died in infancy. Gulian graduated at Columbia College, in 1801, and having studied law, and been admitted to the bar, he opened an office for practice in the city of New York, but his mind was soon turned to political and literary pursuits, in which he became eminent. On the 2d of October, 1811, he was married to " Eliza Fenno, daughter of John Ward and Mary (Curtis) Fenno, originally of Boston, but later of Philadelphia." The voyage to Europe for the recovery of her health failed of its object, and she died of consumption in Paris, April 29, 1817, and was buried in the Cemetery of Père La Chaise. Two children, one in his third year, and the other a babe of six months, had been left behind when the voyage was undertaken. Mr. Verplanck tenderly cherished her memory through life, and did not marry again. His contributions to the literature of his country, and his philanthropic efforts as well, have given him a reputation beyond the bounds of his native State.

He died suddenly in New York, Friday, March 18, 1870, and was buried at Fishkill, where a large estate has been held by the family for several generations.

friends at home were several to Dr. Johnson, and they must have been particularly gratifying to him, who half a century before had himself gone over much of the ground, and noted the peculiarities of the countries and the habits of the people.

The first of these letters produced here was written from

MARSEILLES, *November* 7, 1816.

HONORED SIR, — We arrived at this city four days ago, on our way to Nice, where we intend passing the winter. We left Paris on the 17th October, shortly after the date of my last letter, and travelled south by the way of Champagne, to Lyons. In this city, the second of the now kingdom, and the fourth of the former empire of France, we stayed three days. Its quays and public works are magnificent, but the greatest part of the city presents a scene of squalid misery, which almost made me tremble for the consequences of our manufacturing spirit. There are no great manufacturing establishments in Lyons. The work is given out in what is called piece-work, by the fabricants, and the splendid tapestry and embroidery which decorates St. Cloud, Fontainebleau, the Hague, and St. Petersburg, is all made in the most filthy and miserable garrets of a dark and narrow street in Lyons. We have a phrase in English of " stepping across the street," which in Lyons is literally true; there are many streets of houses five stories high which would not require a long stride to step across. From Lyons we passed down the Eastern bank of the Rhone, as far as the Pont St. Esprit, through a country highly picturesque and rich in wines. The Rhone too affords great facility for forming artificial meadows, and when we passed in the last days of October the farmers were cutting their grass, I suppose, for the fifth or sixth time. I had however seen the system of irrigation carried much further in the valleys of the Pyrenees, but this is almost the only district of France where a good dairy can be found in the neighborhood of vineyards. On our journey we stayed a night at St. Remy, a town of four or five thousand inhabitants, in a country rich in wine and oil, and though we were . at the best and most splendid tavern within thirty miles, we could not get milk or butter enough for a breakfast. Upon the whole it appears to me that the vine and olive are rather the blessings which Providence has bestowed upon a country which would be poor without them, than the proof of a wealthy country. The finest parts of France are those where the vine does not grow, Normandy, Picardy, and Artois. But there are great districts of our country both in climate and soil corresponding to the best wine provinces of France, and if the cultivation of the vine would introduce French temperance among our people, it would be a great benefit to the nation. From Pont St. Esprit we took the road to Nismes, where the Roman remains, and the noble canals and basin of the great fountain (which within thirty feet of its source affords water enough to float a large vessel), afforded us ample reward for having gone a little out of our way. I saw no beggars in Nismes. This singular exception to the general character of the French and Flemish towns is ascribed to the influence of Protestantism. The same thing is remarked wherever the Protestants are predominant in France. In Nismes most of the substantial citizens are Protestant. The people in power, and the very low are, however, Catholic. From Nismes we reached this city by way of Aix, a pretty little city, and for a French town, a very clean one. This city is the great entrepot of Mediterranean commerce, and is filled with Turks, Greeks, Albanians, and all the nations which border the Adriatic and Mediterranean.

Eliza's health is much improved since the summer. She desires to be remembered to all her friends at Stratford. It was her intention to have written my aunt from this port, but she had so much to write her sister and brother that she had deferred it until we arrived at Nice. Besides which no vessel sails from this port for some weeks, which lessens the immediate inducement of writing, and it is probable that my aunt may hear from us by Bordeaux or Havre, before you receive this. My respects to my grandmother and uncle, and remain your affectionate grandson,

G. C. VERPLANCK.

A month after the burial of his wife, whose death in Paris has been noted, he wrote again to Dr. Johnson, this time from London, where he had been diverting his mind by looking in upon the Courts of Law, and observing the spirit of party, both in Church and State. His estimate of judicial dignity and of some of the leading men and measures of that period is worth preserving.

LONDON, *June* 5, 1817.

HONORED SIR, — I arrived here nearly three weeks ago, having crossed from Havre to Southampton. I have been very fortunate in happening to visit London at this season, Parliament being in session, the town very full, and it being term-time, during the first week of my residence here. The Court of King's Bench must present a very different scene now from what you knew it in the time of the dignified and graceful Lord Mansfield. Nothing can be less so than the present Chief Justice; his manner is exceedingly bad, his elocution drawling and inelegant, and his whole behavior undignified. Two of his colleagues, Abbot and Bailey, are probably much abler men than he, and certainly in manner they, especially Bailey, have greatly the advantage. In the Common Pleas, Gibbs presides with great ability; he reminds me much of our Mr. Harrison in manner. I heard a cause tried at Guildhall before each of the Lord Chiefs, and my respect for Ellenborough was by no means increased; he seems petulant, and his charge, though it may have been clear enough, was by no means impressive.

Abbot at the Old Bailey yesterday excited a great storm of popular indignation by a singular stretch of judicial power in a trial for a political libel. The jury had, it seems, in consequence of the opposition of three of them to the rest agreed upon a special verdict, which the foreman began to deliver, saying: Guilty, and then added *but;* the Judge ordered the verdict to be recorded as guilty in spite of the opposition of counsel and the explanation of the jurors.

Everything which bears any relation to politics is carried to excess by both parties. A friend of mine who has long been considered as a violent democrat in Virginia and New York, dined the other day at a reformer's public dinner, Burdett in the chair; many speeches were made, and he came away shocked at what he called the gross ferocious Jacobinism of these men.

I paid a visit of four days to Cambridge, and was much gratified and amused. I had fortunately the means of introduction to some gentlemen of Trinity and St. John's. On Sunday, which was a scarlet day, I saw the University in all its pomp, and heard Dr. Maltby preach before them.

The University like the Church is divided into two parties, which seem to look upon each other with great hostility. In Cambridge, Dr. Maltby is the head of one, and Simeon of the other. As preachers, I was not much struck with either. But the great wonder of London in pulpit oratory at present is Dr. Chalmers, of the Church of Scotland; he is so followed that a ticket to the gallery of one of his charity sermons is as much sought after as one to see Kemble on his taking leave of the stage. I heard him once, and though he has every possible fault of manner and accent, I think he deserves all his popularity; his great characteristic is wonderful ingenuity in argument, which keeps the attention constantly alive, and this is united to great clearness and earnestness. He has lately published an argument on the evidences of Christianity, and a volume of astronomical lectures, both of which have had an unexampled sale.

Every one agrees in the opinion that the state of the country is serious and alarming beyond example. The ministry are resolute in persevering in the present system, and the old opposition is completely broken up; a part of them, such as Brougham and the house of Russell, falling into the ranks of the reformers, and the rest with Lord Grenville partially supporting the ministers. In spite of the clamors about sinecures and pensions the general conviction seems to be that reform in this respect will not alleviate the public burden ; it is war and the consequence of it, the debt under which the nation suffers. The agricultural prospects of the country, both at home and in those countries from which it derives its chief foreign supplies, are understood to be good this year, but the depression of commerce and manufactures continues without any change. My best respects to my grandmother and aunt.

I remain your affectionate grandson,

G. C. VERPLANCK.

Another letter, which appears to have been the last before his return home, was written from

LIVERPOOL, *July* 10, 1817.

HONORED SIR, — I arrived here on my way to the North last Saturday, having stopped on the road for a short time at Oxford and Cheltenham. I was unfortunate in seeing Oxford to the greatest possible disadvantage, it being vacation, and the University perfectly empty. My companion, Dr. Kollock, of Georgia, and myself, had letters to the Professor of Chemistry, to Dr. Barnes, a Canon of Christ Church, who, it is said, will fill the next vacancy on the bench of Bishops, and to several Fellows, but they were all gone, and we were obliged to wander through the stately halls and chapels with a hired University guide. Whether it was from this circumstance I cannot say, but certainly we did not concur in giving Oxford that proud superiority which she claims over the sister University. It is, I think, inferior in walks and gardens, it has no single college superior to Trinity, and no building to be compared with King's Chapel.

Cheltenham is now the fashionable watering place, but my curiosity was soon gratified there, and having no time to spare we left it in twenty-four hours. Thence we took the lower road by Tewkesbury, Worcester (which is, I think, the finest provincial town I have seen), Shrewsbury and Chester. Liverpool is now what Bristol formerly was, the great mart of the American and Colonial trade. It is filled with Americans, and seems busy and prosperous, though the merchants complain loudly. Its curiosities are the docks, which are very fine, and Mr. Roscoe, the banker and author, a very gentlemanly and agreeable man. The country through which I have passed on my road hither is very beautiful. What particularly strikes me is the freshness and soft color of the verdure; the greatest want in the rural scenery of England, to me, is that of fine rivers. After being accustomed to our grand streams I can hardly bring myself to give the name of rivers to such streams as the Severn or the Isis. Though the country surpassed my expectations, the villages disappointed me. They are certainly inferior in beauty and comfort to those of New England, and (except the mere commercial villages as Newburgh, etc.) to those of New York and Jersey.

The Bishop of Chester is now holding a confirmation here, which seems to attract great attention, for the street is completely crowded in front of the Church. Though the brother of Lord Ellenborough, he is said to be a man of little talent. The present bench is not brilliant. The Bishops of Gloucester and Norwich are highly respected for their zeal and piety, and the venerable Bishop of Durham for the princely generosity with which he expends his immense revenues in useful public establishments. The rest appear to be considered as respectable, but rather negative characters, except Dr. Marsh, Watson's successor in the See of Landaff, who is a scholar and a politician, and who is said to have fought his way with his pen to a Bishoprick, and to intend to make himself Primate. He is the champion of one of the parties into which the Church is now unhappily divided, and is as active in inflaming as the Bishop of Gloucester is in soothing these discords. The Dissenters are certainly increasing rapidly, and yet if attachment or dislike of the Liturgy be taken as the test of dissent they are decreasing, for the Liturgy is now used in a very great number of congregations whose chapels are licensed by the Dissenting Act.

Political party runs very high; there is great bitterness on both sides. The ministry have lost by the determined opposition of Lord Wellesley to all their late measures, and have gained on the other hand by the accession of the Grenville party.

There is every prospect of an abundant harvest here, and throughout Europe, and this is looked to by the ministerial men with great confidence, as the certain cure of the present difficulties of the nation, while the opposition regard everything as hopeless without the severest economical reform.

I set out to-morrow for Manchester, thence my plan is to go to Leeds, York, and to Edinburgh. I shall probably cross to Ireland from Scotland, but this must depend on the time I have to spare; my wish is to revisit Holland, and then to return home from the Continent in September or October. I beg to be kindly remembered to my grandmother, uncle, and aunt, and remain your affectionate grandson,

G. C. VERPLANCK.

Mr. Verplanck being a great lover of art and a patron of some of the best American artists of his time, employed John Wesley Jarvis to proceed to Stratford in the autumn of 1814, and paint for him the portrait of his grandfather as he appeared in his latest days. Two pictures were painted, and on the occasion of presenting one of them to his granddaughter,[1] he made this statement in writing: "The two portraits of Dr. Johnson by Jarvis were taken successively in the same month, and are in-

---

[1] *Mary*, now wife of Mr. Samuel William Johnson, Wappinger's Falls, N. Y., a great grandson of the subject of this volume. The companion picture is in the possession of her father, William Samuel Verplanck, Esq., Fishkill-on-Hudson.

tended to exhibit different and marked expressions of the same person. One of them portrays him in an animated conversation; the other gives his habitual meditative expression, whilst his deafness shut out the intrusion of the external world."

As it is natural for a parent to watch the course of the child that has been carefully reared, so Dr. Johnson continued to be interested in the Institution over which, for many years, he had presided with such dignity and acceptance. He kept his eye upon its changes and modifications, and lived to know that all but one or two of his colleagues had either voluntarily relinquished their positions or passed to the grave. It was not long after his retirement to Stratford that a great revolution in the affairs of the College took place, and writing January 22, 1802, to his son, Samuel William Johnson, then at Fayetteville, N. C., he thus described it: "I know not whether you will think it worth while to mention to you that a great revolution has taken place in Columbia College. Dr. Wharton has resigned, and the trustees have appointed Dr. Bowden Professor of Moral Philosophy and Rhetoric, and to do all the presidential duties except at Commencement, with the salary I enjoyed; Bishop Moore to be President, to attend at examinations and preside at Commencement, with a salary of £140, and the graduation fees. And as Dr. Mitchill has gone off to Congress, they intend to supersede him by appointing another Professor of Chemistry in his place. Dr. Bowden has accepted the appointment, and they have had a meeting at Cheshire to provide a successor in the Academy. Dr. Smith, late of Norwalk, is talked of."

Besides being the witness to another war with Great Britain, he was a witness also, in the closing years of his life, to a civil and political revolution in his own State, which overturned the existing order of things, and brought a new party into power that would not rest until the finishing stroke had been given to the intolerance which, for nearly five generations, had been sheltered under the old colonial charter of King Charles the Second. The people had learned to reverence that charter, and prior to the establishment of American Independence, it was viewed as the palladium of their liberties. Hence it was not laid aside, and the new Constitution of 1818 set up in its place, without a fierce and bitter conflict. Sharp pamphlets and sharper contributions to the periodical press appeared during the opening scenes of the conflict, and led to measures which broke down the established ecclesiastical system, and allowed to all the inhabitants of the State equal civil and religious privileges. Perhaps no period of Connecticut history is more important or of more general interest than that which covers the events of this revolution.

It was too late for Dr. Johnson to take an active part in public matters, but whatever may have been his political predilections, he looked quietly on and noted the changes that swept away the charter, for the integrity of which he had contended half a century before while colonial agent in Great Britain. Governor Wolcott said of it in his message to the General Assembly at the May session, 1818: "Considered merely as an instrument defining the powers and duties of magistrates and rulers, this charter may justly be considered as unprovisional and imperfect;

12

yet it ought to be recollected that what is now its greatest defect was formerly a preëminent advantage, — it being then highly important to the people to acquire the greatest latitude and authority with an exemption from British interference and control."

CHAPTER XV.

HAPPY DECLINE; DEATH; AND CHARACTER.

A. D. 1817–1819.

DR. JOHNSON continued in the serene enjoyment of his books and of his religious faith, and with a second wife, whom he had married[1] some time after his retirement to Stratford, his years glided happily on, and he passed beyond his ninety-second birthday. It has been well said, " He that would be long an old man, must begin early to be one,"— a truism which involves the relinquishment of youthful pursuits and habits before the arrival of age, when the natural decay of the faculties is followed for the most part by a stagnation of life.

For years previous to his death, many things conspired to invest his character with a sacredness which almost made him to be regarded as a being belonging to another world, though still lingering on earth. He

---

[1] *Mrs. Mary Beach*, of Kent, Conn., widow of a kinsman of his first wife. Under date of December 8, 1800, he entered in his diary that he set out with his son Charles and a servant in a carriage for Kent, where they arrived the next day at four o'clock. 9th. " Executed contract of marriage to Mrs. Beach. 10th. Set out with Mrs. B—— at ten o'clock, and lodged at Baldwin's, at Newtown. More moderate weather. 11th. Warmer and thawing. Came home at three, and at six o'clock in evening married by the Rev. Mr. Baldwin to Mrs. Beach."

unfolded that constant elevation often observed in the character of good men as they advance in life, until at its close they appear in a measure to have lost the stains of human corruption and to be translated rather than raised by death to immortality.

Some lines from "The Vanity of Human Wishes," a poem written by his illustrious namesake, Dr. Samuel Johnson, the great light of English literature, will describe him very properly as he appeared in his last days : —

> "The virtues of a temperate prime,
> Bless with an age exempt from scorn or crime;
> An age that melts in unperceived decay,
> And glides in modest innocence away;
> Whose peaceful day benevolence endears,
> Whose night congratulating conscience cheers;
> The general favorite as the general friend,
> Such age there is, and who shall wish its end ? "

A gentleman of South Carolina, of high culture and standing, writing to a friend in New York city about the time of Dr. Johnson's decease, thus spoke of him, at the age of ninety : " In the summer of 1817, I visited Stratford, and never shall I forget the delightful hours I passed in the company of your venerable and excellent relative.   He carried me back to his residence in England, and to the company of Johnson, of Mansfield, and of Chatham.   The theme made him eloquent ; and I shall ever consider it a happiness to have heard that eloquence which produced such an impression upon the Royal Council of England. Age, though it had impaired his person, and a little dimmed his eyes, had still left him a voice of the finest tones, which I can never forget." [1]

[1] *Christian Journal*, vol. iii. p. 382.

Similar testimony, borne by others who visited him in his retirement, might be adduced; but enough has been given to satisfy an ordinary curiosity, and complete the story of his eventful life. His death occurred at Stratford, on Sunday, the 14th of November, 1819, two months after he had reached his ninety-second birthday; and he uttered in the end no words but those which evinced a desire for the prosperity of his country and the spread of Christianity. He was buried in the family vault, where the mother of his children, twenty-five years before, had been laid to her rest, and his truest monument is to be seen in the institutions which it was his privilege to have been so instrumental in shaping and advancing.

One little circumstance may here be mentioned to illustrate his religious character. He left behind him in manuscript a book of prayers, which he said was compiled by him in the time of Whitefield, when there was much excitement in the land, and it became necessary for every one in his turn, in the families where he resided, to offer prayer. This book was used to assist his memory, and that he might be prepared to offer nothing improper, or inconsistent with the rules of the Episcopal Church, in which, from early life, he had been a devout communicant.

There are passages in these prayers which have a strange sound to us at the present day, such as the following, which appear to have been repeated in the time of the old French War in Canada : " Bless thy universal Church, and preserve it from all error. Defend the Protestant cause. Preserve the life of our sovereign, King George: Bless his counsels at home and his arms abroad, and give to him, and all other Christian kings, princes, governors, magistrates, and ministers, both of State and religion, wisdom, virtue, and integrity, and make them real blessings to mankind in the exalted stations they possess. Send thy blessing upon the British nation and colonies in general, and this colony in particular. Defend us from our enemies now in arms against us, and give us to triumph over them, and to reduce them to reasonable terms of peace."

Such a man, living at any time, is a great blessing to his country, but a greater still when he lives in a period of national emergencies that demand the most enlightened judgment, and the soundest principles of political wisdom and virtue. Dr. Johnson had extraordinary opportunities to acquire the knowledge necessary to fit him for a noble actor in critical and troublous times, and it was his good fortune for the most part to be joined in council with those who appreciated his dignity and attainments and honored the spirit by which he was actuated. He was a wise statesman who favored high maxims of government and cultivated broad and liberal views. With a vigorous intellect, trained in the contests of a stirring life, he was wont to do for his country under all circumstances precisely what he believed to be for its true interest and advancement among the nations of the earth. His long residence abroad did not make him any the less an American, though it may have taught him, as already shown, in view of the weakness of the Colonies, to place a higher value upon the lessons of prudence and moderation.

When he wrote to Richard Jackson two years after his return home, and gave a gloomy picture of the

tumults in this country growing out of what were
considered to be the cruelty and injustice of the
Ministry, and mentioned the first meeting of a "numerous Congress" of all the Colonies in Philadelphia,
to concert measures of defense, he added : " I have,
in pursuance of your good advice, endeavored carefully to persuade our people to be calm and moderate,
and to prevent their running into mobs and extrava-
gances. Some success I have had ; I wish I could
say nothing of this nature had happened amongst us,
but they have not hitherto been very violent. And
though a moderator is indeed a very unpopular character at present, I am resolved to adhere to it, and
do everything possible to keep the ardor of my
countrymen within bounds, though it is more than
probable that I shall thereby forfeit their esteem."

This was the spirit of Dr. Johnson in reference to
the disputes between the two countries which led to
the Revolution ; and yet when he was measuring
lances with Lord Hillsborough, and contending for
the rights of Connecticut under the Charter of King
Charles the Second, he was prepared to lay aside that
spirit, and said to him : " I hope that England will not
add to our burdens ; you certainly would find it re-
dound to your own prejudice." He was a statesman
who seemed never to have allowed personal considerations for a single moment to swerve him from the
strict line of duty. Not an instance can be cited to
show that he was ever governed by sinister motives,
or endeavored to accomplish an object by dishonor-
able means. Loyal to truth and to the honest con-
victions of his own mind, he shrunk from any deception, and brushed away those seductive influences

which too often warp the judgment of men in public station.

As far back as 1772, when writing to his friend Robert Temple, and encouraging him in his gloomy apprehensions to submit to the dispensations of Providence, he said : " For my part, I have seen so much of the follies of the world, particularly the political part of it, ... that I am heartily sick of politics, and am endeavoring to forget all I have observed upon that subject ; to erase from my mind every political idea as relative to the present conduct of affairs, and to attend to my own duty only as a Christian, a man, and a member of society. When iniquity abounds, the love of many will wax cold. Iniquity does now abound : let us take care that our Christianity, though put to the test, as I doubt not yours has sufficiently been, be not shaken, and that our love for things really good wax not cold."

His advancement to great honors was not the result of political management, but rather the spontaneous tribute of an appreciative and grateful people. Nor did he cling to these honors as if they were his life. He was ready to relinquish them for others less exalted, and perhaps less remunerative. Four months after his election to the presidency of Columbia College, he wrote from New York to his son, then at Bermuda: " I am now to decide with respect to the presidency of the College here, which I am much pressed to accept. I am yet undetermined, as the support is very moderate, and I must give up every other prospect." At the age of sixty, he took the office of a college president, and resigned henceforth all expectations of political preferment, not knowing at

that time that his native Connecticut would still seek
his services by choosing him to be her first Senator
in Congress, according to the provisions of the new
Federal Constitution which he had helped to frame
and put in force.

Very little has been preserved of his forensic efforts,
or of his speeches in deliberative assemblies and the
Senate of the United States. Had he done what others since his time have done so extensively, — written out his arguments and carefully revised them for
the press, — it is quite certain he would have added
to his literary reputation, and enrolled his name
among those distinguished orators and diplomatists
whose published works are a most valuable part of
the legacy bequeathed to their country. Eloquence
gathered in public records and enshrined in the pages
of history, will not have all the force and freshness of
the living orator, but it will still speak to the under-
standings of men in times of stormy agitation and
bewildering excitement, as well as in quiet and un-
eventful periods. The knowledge of constitutional
law and the philosophy of government must be acquired by studying the best models and becoming
familiar with the productions of the most eminent
jurists and legislators of past generations.

But the crowning feature in the character of Dr.
Johnson was his Christian faith. It has been seen in
these pages how reverently he worshiped God, and
how firmly he believed in those truths of Divine revelation which are not only the support of the individual soul, but the strong foundation on which to
build the government and laws of a country. He
had a keen perception of what he dwelt upon in his

public addresses to the graduating classes of Columbia
College, that the first great duty of a man is owed to
Heaven, to his Creator and Redeemer; and he prac-
ticed that duty in all the posts of honor and responsibility which he was called to fill. He was on this
account the more noble. For a Christian statesman
is the glory of his age, and the memory of his deeds
and virtues will reflect a light coming from a source
which neither clouds can dim nor shadows obscure.

Born in a period of religious history when the
Puritanism of Connecticut was most intolerant, and
taught by a parent who had learned to battle well for
Episcopacy, he became warmly attached to the distinguishing principles of the Church of England, and
like his father was of the school of Andrewes, of
Leslie, of Potter, of Horne, of Jones of Nayland, and
of Horsley. In his enlightened mind, however, these
principles were not embraced from the prejudices of
education, or from reverence of parental authority;
but they were the result of an investigation which he
did not deem beneath the powers of his acute and
vigorous intellect. He had been on intimate terms
with some of the greatest and best laymen of England, and however much he might have disliked the
policy of the British government towards his own
country, and the State religion which for a long time
refused it the Episcopacy, he yet loved the Church,
which he considered as a divinely constituted society
under Jesus Christ its head.

As in civil, so in ecclesiastical matters, his knowledge and experience were highly serviceable to the
Episcopalians of Connecticut in assisting them, after
the Revolution, to organize and adapt themselves to

their new political condition. When Seabury was in London, trying to feel and find his way through the Parliamentary impediments which surrounded him, he wrote home to his friends, and, for the purpose of removing from the minds of English prelates one great obstacle to his consecration, suggested that application should be made to the General Assembly for permission to have a Bishop reside in the State. Dr. Johnson, being then in the full practice of his profession, interpreted for the clergy the general law which had been passed, embracing the Episcopal Church, and comprehending all the legal rights and powers intended to be given to any denomination of Christians. The permission sought for was in his view, as in the view of other civilians, quite unnecessary, for opposition to the residence of a Bishop in Connecticut, whatever strength it had before the separation of the Colonies from the mother country, was no longer a reality, and could not be set up with any show of reason. The very idea of it was inconsistent with the principles of civil and religious liberty aimed at in the establishment of American Independence.

It is often a difficult thing for the men of one household of faith fully to understand and appreciate those of another. Bigotry and intolerance naturally grow out of such misconception and acquire force, until knowledge comes in to help the recognition of truth and the practice of duty. Dr. Johnson had mixed too much with the world, and seen too much of every phase of society, to be of an illiberal spirit. He never appears to have forgotten that those of opposite sentiments have precisely the same excuse for unbending firmness that they have for inbred dislike

of adverse doctrines. On religious subjects he cour-
teously paid that deference to the opinions of others
which he claimed for his own, and was ready as a
public man, and as occasion required, to act in defense of individuals from whom he widely differed.
He had been a witness to so much bitter controversy
in his father's day, that, judging from his letters, he
seemed more inclined to sympathize with goodness
wherever he found it than to engage in the discussion of doctrinal or ecclesiastical questions.

His polished humor sometimes cut deep like the
wit of Sydney Smith. When the clergy of Connecticut, after the death of Bishop Jarvis, were unable
to agree upon a successor, and several Conventions
had been held without effecting an election, he was
gravely asked if he would not name a suitable candidate — some person of fine culture and shining abilities, eloquent as a preacher and attractive as a man
— who might be chosen to fill the vacancy. And he
replied that he thought " they had better elect his
friend Dr. Dwight." [1]

The Church was the subject of his thoughts, and
worship in the sanctuary a source of enjoyment to
him in his closing years, for when, through the infirmities of age, he could no longer put forth active
efforts in its behalf, he was wont to manifest the
deepest interest in its state and prosperity. Other
men in his physical condition might have sought
more privacy, and preferred the solitude of their
chambers for religious meditation ; but though un-

---

[1] A Congregational divine, and President of Yale College, whose published works in prose and poetry have given his name a high place in the
literature of his country.

able to hear sermons, Dr. Johnson continued to frequent the house of God, and it is recorded of him that he united with the congregation in the prayers of the Liturgy with the most reverent and edifying devotion. He was a layman of whom his Church, like his country, might well be proud; and there is nothing, perhaps, in the whole of his varied and distinguished career more to be admired than the perfect beauty of his quiet and saintly life at Stratford.

The example of his character not only commends itself to the imitation of those in public positions, but it has a voice of instruction for young men in every age who seek patterns of truth, of honor, of justice, of love and faith. Moral qualities are best seen and appreciated when presented in human forms. The history of nations is but the history of men — of rulers of the people and leading characters who figure in the different departments of patriotism, government, learning, science, philosophy, art, and commerce, so that the faults to be avoided and the virtues to be cultivated are substantially the same in each generation.

Few indeed are they who will not be made wiser by contemplating the conduct of those who have trodden the noble paths in which they themselves aspire to tread, and fewer still, perhaps, to whom such examples will not afford a just encouragement. Young men, who feel the impulses of an honorable ambition in life; who are determined to be useful to their fellow-beings according to their ability, and to increase their ability by diligent self-culture and the practice of every virtue, will most surely fail to accomplish their lofty object unless they breathe a

healthy intellectual atmosphere, and reject teachings
that lead away from the beaten tracks of goodness
and greatness. The exclamation which fell from the
lips of Aaron Burr, at the close of his notorious life.
was alike full of truth and of pathos: " Had I read
Voltaire less, I should have known that the world
was wide enough for Hamilton and me." Every
moral truth is deepened when seen in the light of
God, and the higher grades of human character are
not formed by shutting out this light and dwelling in
darkness and doubt.

There is need in our day of a more elevated public opinion, of more profound respect for religion, and
of greater regard for the authority of law and the
dictates of conscience. In the chase after wealth, or
honor, or pleasure, or power, a high standard is too
frequently overlooked, and means to gain an end
adopted which dwarf all the actings of the intellect,
and thrust from view the sense of moral obligation.
Though society be ever changing and new combina-
tions of circumstances perpetually occurring, yet there
are certain general principles which are of universal
application, and the neglect of these, to any great
extent, among the thinking, educated classes of the
community is pretty sure to be followed by unhappy
consequences. A school of reckless, daring men, to
whom duty supported by religion is no chosen guide,
may make a name for itself in history, but it will not
be a name to be covered with lasting honor and
glory.

Whether in the strife for political ascendency and
power, or in calmer pursuits, in the tranquil walks of
science and literature, the one thing to be remem-

bered and sought after is the service of God, in maintaining the standard of moral excellence and promoting the advancement and happiness of the human race. Not all are equally well situated for this service. Public life, for example, has its grievous and manifold temptations, and the time of statesmen is usually so much absorbed in national subjects and the schemes of official policy, that little room is left for quiet and sober reflection upon religious truth and duty. Great characters were grouped around the throne of George the Third, but they were so intent on saving the Colonies to the kingdom, and on asserting the power of the government and its right to tax subjects without allowing them representation, that they could not see where the lines of honor and justice ran, and so became the promoters of a seven years' war, which, viewed at the distance of a century, reflects no glory upon the English nation.

American youth who study the history of their country will find among the great men who assisted in laying the foundations of our Republic many who were controlled by the sternest rules of political integrity, and by Christian principle as well, and among these stands the name of WILLIAM SAMUEL JOHNSON. The simple story of his life as now told will revive the memory of his virtues, and open up his character to the better acquaintance of readers of American history.

APPENDIX.

13

APPENDIX A.

THE determination of Connecticut to resist the Stamp Act was foreshadowed by Johnson in the following letter, written after the action of the General Assembly upon the petitions agreed to by the Congress. Many members took exception to the manner of acknowledging the "subordination" of the Colonies to Parliament, but the Petitions, without alteration, were approved by a large majority.

TO JAMES OTIS, ESQ., BOSTON.

DEAR SIR, — I have the pleasure to inform you that the Petitions agreed to by the Congress have been approved by the General Assembly of this Colony, ordered to be signed by their Commissioners, and forwarded by his Honor, the Governor. Even *due subordination* passed. They were not indeed in this respect as well as in some others, perfectly such as they would have wished, but a union of the Petitioning Colonies, even in language as well as sentiment, was justly thought of more importance than mode of expression or elegance of diction. We truly represented to the House that taking all circumstances into consideration, the Congress could make them no better than they are.

After much debate it was concluded not to appoint a new agent upon this business, but special instructions were given to Mr. Jackson to prefer these Petitions, and he is engaged not to admit the power of Parliament, but on all proper occasions to insist upon the exclusive right of the Colonies to tax themselves and the privilege of trial by jury, as principles which we cannot depart from.

The Stamp paper is not yet come into the Colony, but we are very generally agreed to submit to all the inconveniences of a total stagnation of business rather than admit the Act: indeed, many are for proceeding in everything as usual, and taking no notice at all of it, but I fancy we shall lie still for the present.

It would give me particular pleasure to know what reception the Petitions meet with at your Assembly, what you do in regard to an agent, and any other steps taken in this most important affair by your very respectable House of Representatives ; and I am with the greatest esteem and regard, sir,

Your most obedient and very humble servant.

STRATFORD, *Novr. 4th*, 1765.

APPENDIX B.

ROBERT TEMPLE and John, a younger brother, — afterwards Sir John Temple, — were both in England during the agency of Dr. Johnson. He entered in his Diary under date of Feb. 19th, 1767, ten days after his arrival in London, that he "went with Temple by water to London Bridge," and from that time to the 24th of the following September, they were much in each other's company. The Diary begins again with mentions of Mr. Temple, on Saturday, 29th of December, 1770, and a week later it is entered: "In evening received a long visit from Mr. Temple, who stayed till 11 o'clock." The Christian name is nowhere used to designate the person. This must be determined by other evidence, and the first letter below will prove that it was *Robert* who accompanied him in 1767, having placed his son of the same name at school in Norwich before he returned to America. The other, with letters printed in the body of the work, will show that Robert was not in England in 1771, but that his brother *John* was there, and had obtained an official position under the Crown.

TO ROBERT TEMPLE, ESQ.

LONDON, *November* 20, 1767.

DEAR SIR, — Before this time I hope you are in full possession of all the joys of Ten Hills, and that your passage to that scene of all your wishes has been more agreeable than your fears or the fullness of the ship prognosticated. Nothing very material has happened here worth mentioning to you, for I presume you will have heard of the death of the Duke of York and the birth of another prince, and must have earlier and fuller accounts of Colonel Shirley's success than I can give you. Everything, he tells me, has turned out to his wish, and I assure you I take as sincere a part in this good fortune of his as any of his friends, being, as I have told you, in my opinion, not only due to his merits, but in strict justice to the family, which has been but very illy rewarded for their services to the Crown.

You will not expect I can tell you anything material relative to politics before Parliament meets, which, however, will now be very soon. Lord North is Chancellor of Exchequer, and it is said Lord Chatham is recovered and will again engage in business, — the last, however, is doubted; no speedy change of administration is at present expected. Mr. W. was much pleased with your honest letter, as he called it, from Canterbury, and showed it, he told me, to Mrs. Grenville, the first time he saw her, who was equally pleased, and retains much regard for you, as do all your friends.

For myself, I assure you, I found myself much alone after your departure, and in a week's time set out on my northern tour, which served for amusement at the same time that it contributed so much to the recovery of my health, which I thank God is now very well restored.

At Norwich I had the pleasure to see your pretty son in full health, fine spirits, cheerful and happy, and to find him, in my opinion, in good hands. Mr. Mego is exactly the man you described him ; learned, diligent, perfectly well-disposed, and honest, but equally unpolished and unpracticed in the ways of the world, which, however, by no means derogates from his real worth as a clergyman and a preceptor ; in the latter of which characters you are much interested in him, and I flatter myself he will not disappoint your expectations. His lady and daughter are on the contrary suffi-

ciently polished and conversable, and will answer all your
purposes of politeness, so that taking all the family together
they have all the qualities, I think, requisite for this early
stage of your son's education.

I was much pleased with Norwich, its cathedral, castle, etc.
When I was at Lady Leicester's and Houghton Hall, I re-
gretted much that you had left England without seeing these
two magnificent seats. The grand and elegant architecture
of the one and the admirable pictures of the other, exceed
all description, and are, I believe, as much worth seeing as
anything in England. The Cathedrals of Lincoln, York,
and Peterborough are certainly very fine, but after having
seen Canterbury, Westminster Abbey, etc., one has so good
an idea of that species of buildings that there is no great
reason to regret the not having seen a greater number of
them. Lady Leicester's and Houghton Hall are originals,
and so peculiarly excellent that I strongly wished you had
visited them. Be sure you don't forget to see them the *next*
time you come to England.

Since I came to town I have been but once into the City,
but spend almost all my time in Westminster Hall, and believe shall continue that course through the winter. Now
and then I go to a Play with Palmer (who, by the way, being
disappointed of Mr. Wentworth's company, has given up
the thoughts of going abroad this winter) and thus I while
away the time till, like you, I can return to my dear native
country, family, and friends, from whom I think no consideration shall ever again so long separate me.

Mr. Apthorp, though better, is not yet recovered, and is
gone to try the effects of certain waters in Derbyshire by
advice of Dr. Fothergil. It is said there are some warm
pieces in your late papers. I have not seen them yet, but
Whately says they are treasonable, and if they were here,
the printers and publishers would certainly be punished.
We are impatient to know what reception the Board meets
with, and what in general is the state of political affairs in
Boston, which you will be sure to let us know, as anything

material occurs. Present my compliments to your brother and Mr. Hutton, Paxton, etc., and to your lady and family whom though I have not the honor to know, yet from the affection I have for you I seem to have some interest in.

Upon looking back I see this is a most insignificant letter, and tells you nothing of any kind of importance. Charge this, however, to that barrenness of events since you left us, and let it at least serve to assure you that I am with the most sincere esteem,

Your affectionate friend and very humble servant.

P. S. .... Poor Captain Robinson died lately of the small-pox. How hard has been his fate! Driven from his own country by oppression to find his grave in this.

STRATFORD, February 10, 1772.

MY DEAR SIR, — I return you my hearty thanks for your very obliging favor of the 20th of January and for the packet and letters forwarded from your worthy brother, for which I beg you will also return him my thanks when you write him. It was business alone that induced me, contrary to my interest, to return to America, by way of New York. I always resolved, as you recollect, to have taken my passage to Boston, that I might have had the great pleasure to have seen once more, you and my other friends there. When I shall have that pleasure, now I know not, as the necessity of my affairs obliges me, for the support of a numerous family, to engage again deeply in the business of my profession, which in this country leaves a man no leisure for amusement, or tours of pleasure.

I long greatly to see you, and wish most heartily with you that kind Providence had placed us nearer together; but that God in whose hands are all our ways sees, and will do what is best for us; to his dispensations let us submit with all cheerfulness. For my part I have seen so much of the follies and villanies of the world, particularly the political part of it, where, as you justly remark, the practice is still

the good of the public and the support of Government, while
the real object is wealth, or power, or some other dirty selfish
view, that I am heartily sick of politics and am endeavoring
to forget all I have observed upon that subject; to erase
from my mind every political idea as relative to the present
conduct of affairs; and to attend to my own duty only as a
Christian, a man, and a member of society. When iniquity
abounds the love of many will wax cold. Iniquity does
now abound; let us take care that our Christianity (though
put to the test as I doubt not yours has sufficiently been),
be not in any degree shaken, and that our love for those
things that are really good wax not cold. Most of those
things are not worth a wise man's care, and a day of retribu-
tion is at hand when all those apparently perverse things will
be set right to universal satisfaction.

But to return from this preachment. I have seen with
real concern the injustice done to your brother, and heartily
hope he will prevail against his enemies. I was flattered
with the expectation that he would have been appointed one
of the Commissioners of Customs in Ireland, a place of
£1,000 per annum with valuable perquisites, which was a
thing talked of when I left England, but since I hear Governor Bernard is in that Commission I fear that is at an end,
as I apprehend your brother's delicacy will not permit him
to accept a seat at the same board with that gentleman.
Something else, I hope, will turn up equally acceptable.

Your not having heard lately from our friend, Mr.
Whately, is, I hope, owing to his want of leisure, not to any
coldness, for he always expressed great regard for you. He
has been ever since Mr. Grenville's death altogether attached
to Administration. That gentleman's decease, whose fortunes they had followed, he and his intimate friends considered as a total release from their obligations to the Opposition, and thinking it necessary to provide for themselves, they
embarked instantly with Administration. Mr. Whately was
accordingly, you know, immediately made one of the Lords
of Trade, and as soon as his friend Lord Suffolk became

Secretary of State, was appointed his first Secretary and Surveyor of the King's Private Roads, the latter office alone being equal in value to his seat at the Board of Trade. He is, therefore, now quite the man of business, and has not that leisure to see, or to correspond with his friends that he used to have.

My daughter Nancy remembers with pleasure the very agreeable hours she passed at Ten Hills, and joins Mrs. Johnson and me in most affectionate compliments to Mrs. Temple, your daughters, and you; and I remain always, dear sir,

Your very affectionate friend and humble servant.

APPENDIX C.

Dear Sir, — The death of your truly venerable and much respected father in a manner so suitable to the goodness of his heart, and the piety and integrity of his whole life, looks more like the flight of Elijah to the mansions of bliss than the melancholy departure of souls less pure and innocent. Nature will force a tender sigh and filial tear ; but reason bids us approve of the death of the righteous as a passage to everlasting repose. Does reason dictate such consolation ? No, my dear sir, I retract the proud expression. It is revelation, divine revelation, which affords us this healing balm when despair and anguish seize the soul at the parting knell of our beloved friends. This heavenly gift dispels the gloomy doubts and fears which perplexed the wise and learned of antiquity, and this alone brings life and immortality to light.

Your father, whose every word and action was benevolence itself, during his residence here, acquired, nay commanded, the love and esteem of all who had the honor of his acquaintance. The severity of letters, or of age, was no bar to an intimacy with a soul which embraced in fond affection the whole human race. Good humor, affability and condescension, cheerfulness, and an uncommon liberality of sentiment, sweetened every conversation, rendered instruction pleasing, and attracted the love and confidence of the most unthinking. It is no wonder then that I had some place in his friendship, joined as we were in supporting an injured College against the furious attacks of malevolent adversaries; and yet I must confess that I feel more comfort at his leaving the world with calmness and serenity, an ease and composure worthy of the dignity of his character, and the kindness of his life, than distress at a separation which his venerable years rendered unavoidable.

To you, my dear sir, it must give the most substantial satisfaction to reflect that the most inveterate bigot regarded him with reluctant admiration, and the most abandoned profligate revered him for virtues, which though they could not imitate, they were obliged to applaud.

The pathetic manner in which you advocate the cause of the people of Hinsdale does honor to the known goodness of your heart. I can only say that I am much concerned for their misfortune: but looking upon it, for the reasons I assigned, to be irretrievable, I sincerely wish they would embrace Colonel Howard's proposals. They will assuredly find delays to be dangerous: when the Colonel leaves this, which will be soon, their hopes of accommodation must vanish. He very lately expressed much chagrin at the indifference with which they appear to contemplate what he, and all here conceive a very generous offer. Governor Hutchinson has wrote to Governor Tryon in their favor; but placed their defence on a footing very trivial, (to wit) "an argument between Massachusetts and New Hampshire previous to the settlement of their contested boundary in 1739, that the alteration of jurisdiction should not affect private property." But how can such a stipulation affect lands twenty miles to the westward of Mason's grant, which were not in controversy, and which were determined to lie in neither of the contending Colonies? On receiving Governor Tryon's answer with a state of the case, and one of the proclamations, Governor Hutchinson candidly confessed, that they left the Government of New Hampshire, and the claimants under it, without excuse; and assured his Excellency that he should never interpose further in any respect, and that he had acquainted Mr. Hunt, and Mr. Jones, an attorney who accompanied him to Boston, to that effect.

I am much pleased that Governor Tryon's proclamation states the conduct of New Hampshire with respect to us in such a light as to leave them in your opinion also without excuse. I wish it may have its proper weight with the people of Barrington, for whom principally it was intended. They have proceeded to such unwarrantable excesses that I fear their destruction will be inevitable. They have already appeared in arms against the posse of Albany County to prevent the course of Justice, and, it is now reported, are training themselves to have a new conflict with the militia or military, if they should be called upon to support the law's authority, which is found already too weak to encounter their madness. And what is most surprising, these violent measures they have been hurried into in the defence of the possession of one Breckenridge, which lies within seventeen miles of Hudson's River, and beyond any claim which the Government of New Hampshire ever pretended to. If you inquire what can induce them to act so rashly, they justify themselves under *your* letter, and an assurance that ultimately the country will be given back to New Hampshire; and persist in it that they will fight for their possessions. What can be done with these unhappy men? To suffer the course of justice longer to be trampled upon will render Government ridiculous and contemptible. To have recourse to arms is shocking to humanity. If they consulted their true interest, and would be calm and temperate, everybody here would befriend them. The proprietors of the land would give them easy terms; or the Government equivalent lands, plenty of which are yet ungranted. I am sure everything would be accommodated justly, and to the satisfaction of any reasonable mind; and the sufferers of them might be made whole. I never heard a proprietor insinuate that he wished to take the least advantage of their improvements. But alas! if force is used, and they are defeated, — and defeated they must be, — their ruin, I should think, would be complete. I assure you there is nothing gives me more concern than these deluded and infatuated people; the chief of whom have intruded upon these lands with their eyes open, and in the face of proclamations warning and forbidding them ; though undoubtedly some have been abused by the chicane of the Government of New Hampshire, and suffer for their simplicity.

I see you are launched again into the painful Folios of our profession, — for is it not, after all, a farce to spend one's life in an unentertaining drudgery, which affords no other profit than an envied subsistence, and constantly exhibits a melancholy picture of the arts and frauds of our fellow crea- tures, impressing us with the truth of that mortifying ejacu- lation of the poet : *oh ! auri sacra fames, quid non mortalia pectora cogis ?*

Mrs. Duane joins me in respectful compliments to yourself, and Mrs. Johnson. I entreat you to believe that with the warmest regard, I remain, dear sir,

Your most obedient and humble servant,

JAS. DUANE.

NEW YORK, *February* 18, 1772.

STRATFORD, *March* 16, 1772.

MY DEAR SIR, — My attendance on our Superior Court in an interior part of the country deprived me of the pleasure of your favor of the 18th February, till this morning. I now thank you very sincerely for the kind and tender regard you express for the memory of my Father, who had also a most hearty affection and esteem for you ; and am extremely pleased with those noble Christianlike sentiments which you so elegantly express upon occasion of his death. Such senti- ments can be dictated only by that true Christian philosophy which elevates human nature to the highest perfection it is capable of in this state, and prepares it for consummate felicity in the future stages of its existence. I could not as a man, but feel very tenderly the loss of such a Father and friend, yet I agree with you, that we had much more reason to re- joice in the noble manner in which he finished his course and triumphed over the King of Terrors, than occasion to mourn his departure at so advanced an age. I saw it in that light and it afforded me a noble consolation. His exit was precisely such as a wise and good man would wish for.

Let us, my friend, imitate his virtues, that we also may be partakers of that joy which through Faith and Patience he has inherited.

I am very glad you take in good part the concern I expressed for the poor people of Hinsdale. Let me trespass a moment further upon your good nature. The people of Hinsdale, if they had not a legal title to their township — yet in consideration of their early settlement of the country, their long possession and their two mistaken grants from the Crown, had at least an equitable right to the lands ; and in my opinion ought to have received a confirmation without fee or reward under the seal of New York, whose jurisdiction they acknowledge and to whose laws they are willing to be obedient, instead of having a mandamus located upon their lands. Their case, therefore, seems to me to be extremely hard, nor do I well conceive how Colonel Howard can be thought by gentlemen in New York to have made them a very generous offer.

Justice must precede generosity.

Who is Colonel Howard, and what are his services, that he should be entitled to the sweat and labor of these poor people ? He knew, when he laid on his mandamus, that they were in possession of the lands. He did it with his eyes open, and how he can ever reconcile it to his conscience, as an honest man, or to his feelings, as a man of honor, to give so much distress to so many innocent people — I know not. There were vacant lands enough for him to have taken up his grant in ; and to demand a large consideration for quitting to the inhabitants their possession, which he should never have meddled with, appears to me too like the generosity of him who demands one half the money in your purse, as a reward for sparing the remainder — he is sure it is generous, but after all it is the generosity of the highwayman, for which he ought to be hanged.

I have no doubt, if the people of Hinsdale were in a con-

dition to represent their unfortunate case to His Majesty —
the father of his people — and to his ministers, that Colonel
Howard would be ordered to locate his lands somewhere else,
and receive a severe reprimand for the trouble he has given
them. But what can they do at this distance from the throne,
which they cannot approach but at an expense which would
ruin them. Must they submit to injustice, under the spe-
cious name of generosity? They must probably do so!

I saw Mr. Hunt last week at Hartford, who told me he
intended to set out next week for New York to know their
final fate; and I leave them to Providence — and to you.

It gives me real concern that the people of Bennington
should pretend to justify their intemperate and ill-advised
proceedings under a letter from me.

You may rely upon it, they have not, nor ever had any
letter of mine save only a copy of one I wrote in June last
to one of my neighbors, interested in those lands, which contains only a simple relation of the intelligence I had then received from one of the Lords of Trade, of the substance of
the report they had agreed to make, relative to the New
Hampshire lands (with which the report itself, which I
afterwards saw, generally corresponded), the substance of
which as relative to them, was only that the grantees under
New Hampshire who had actually settled their lands, and
done their duty according to the tenor of their grant, should
be quieted; but mentions not a word about the lands being
given back again to New Hampshire. Nor have I since my
return given any man the least reason to expect anything of
that nature; on the contrary I have assured all that I have
seen that there was not the least probability of it, and have
advised them all to pay obedience to the laws of the province of New York and to apply for grants under that government, which many of them I know have accordingly done.
So little ground have these people for the pretense that I
have given any ground for the disobedience to law and disregard to authority which it seems they have been guilty of.
I have therefore nothing to say for them, unless it be, that

perhaps it may be prudent not to proceed to extremities with them until you know the event of the report of the Board of Trade, relative to the settlement of that country, which will probably put an end to their hopes of further arbitration, and perhaps induce them to a quiet submission to the laws. In the mean time I should be extremely glad to know what is the intention of His Excellency Governor Tryon, with regard to granting these lands.

Frequent applications are made to me by the proprietors under New Hampshire, and I wish to be able to give them such information as may be of real use to them. I am particularly concerned for the inhabitants of a town called Norwich, who appear to be very honest people and disposed to do everything fit for them to do, to secure their lands, but extremely ignorant what course they should pursue for that purpose. They have, indeed, sent a person down to New York, who has prepared a petition to the Governor and Council, but hardly know what answer he has received or what they were further to do.

Will you be so kind, dear sir, as to acquaint me what may be depended upon in this matter, and what can be done to secure to these people their lands, who are willing to submit to the laws, and to do anything that can be reasonably required of them, and will be totally ruined if they are turned out of their possessions. I received some time ago, about £30, in New York money, on a bond due to my late brother Nicoll's estate, which I hear with pleasure, is under your conduct. Shall I send it to you, or will it be wanted here for the support of Harry at the College?

Mrs. Johnson joins me in sincere compliments to Mrs. Duane, and I remain with the utmost regard and esteem,

Dear sir, your most obedient

and most humble servant,

WM. SAML. JOHNSON.

To JAMES DUANE, Esq.

14

APPENDIX D.

———•———

HARTFORD, *April* 28 (26 ?), 1775.

SIR, — The alarming situation of public affairs in this country, and the late unfortunate transactions in the Province of Massachusetts Bay, have induced the General Assembly of this Colony, now sitting in this place, to appoint a committee of their body to wait upon your Excellency, and to desire me, in their name, to write to you, relative to those very interesting matters.

The inhabitants of this Colony are intimately connected with the people of your Province, and esteem themselves bound, by the strongest ties of friendship as well as common interest, to regard with attention whatever concerns them. You will not, therefore, be surprised that your first arrival at Boston with a body of His Majesty's troops for the declared purpose of carrying into execution certain Acts of Parliament, which, in their apprehension, are unconstitutional and oppressive, should have given the good people of this Colony a very just and general alarm. Your subsequent proceedings in fortifying the town of Boston, and other military preparations, greatly increased their apprehensions for the safety of their friends and brethren. They could not be unconcerned spectators of their sufferings in that which they esteemed the common cause of this country ; but the late hostile and secret inroads of some of the troops under your command into the heart of the country, and the violences they have committed have driven them almost to a state of desperation. They feel now, not only for their friends, but for themselves and their dearest interests and connections.

We wish not to exaggerate ; we are not sure of every part of our information, but by the best intelligence that we have yet been able to obtain, the late transaction was a most unprovoked attack upon the lives and property of His Majesty's subjects ; and it is represented to us that such outrages have been committed as would disgrace even barbarians, and much more Britons, so highly famed for humanity as well as bravery. It is feared, therefore, that we are devoted to destruction, and that you have it in command and intention to ravage and desolate the country. If this is not the case, permit us to ask, why have these outrages been committed ? Why all the hostile preparations that are daily making ? And why do we continually hear of fresh destinations of troops to this country ? The people of this Colony, you may rely upon it, abhor the idea of taking up arms against the troops of their Sovereign, and dread nothing so much as the horrors of a civil war. But, sir, at the same time we beg leave to assure your Excellency, that as they apprehend themselves justified by the principle of self-defense, they are most firmly resolved to defend their rights and privileges to the last extremity ; nor will they be restrained from giving aid to their brethren, if any unjustifiable attack is made upon them.

Be so good, therefore, as to explain yourself upon this most important subject, so far as is consistent with your duty to our common Sovereign. Is there no way to prevent this unhappy dispute from coming to extremities ? Is there no alternative but absolute submission or the desolations of war ? By that humanity which constitutes so amiable a part of your character, and for the honor of our Sovereign and the glory of the British Empire we entreat you to prevent it if possible. Surely it is to be hoped that the temperate wisdom of the Empire might even yet find expedients to restore peace, that so all parts of the Empire may enjoy their particular rights, honors, and immunities. Certainly this is an event most devoutly to be wished ; and will it not be consistent with your duty to suspend the operations of war on your part, and enable us on ours to quiet the minds of the people, at least till the result of some further deliberations may be known ?

The importance of the occasion will, no doubt, sufficiently apologize for the earnestness with which we address you, and any seeming impropriety which may attend it, as well as induce you to give us the most explicit and favorable answer in your power.

I am, with great esteem and respect, in behalf of the General Assembly, sir, your most obedient servant.

To his Excellency THOMAS GAGE, Esq.

General Gage made a brief reply, and transmitted "a circumstantial account of an unhappy affair," as he termed it, that "happened" in Massachusetts between His Majesty's troops and the people of the country, "whereby," he added, "you will see the pitch their leaders have worked them up to, even to commit hostilities upon the King's troops when an opportunity offered. It has long been said that this was their plan, and so it has turned out."

Governor Trumbull's letter and General Gage's answer are printed in "American Archives," vol. ii., pp. 433–439. The letter has been copied from this volume, where it is preceded by the statement, "Read before Congress, May 19, 1775."

INDEX.

A.

Abbott, Justice, 171.
Act of Parliament, 43.
Adams, John, 110, 112.
Albemarle, Earl of, 63.
Allen, Ebenezer, 113.
America, 39, 41–45, 49, 53, 55–57, 59, 64, 70, 73, 75, 77–79, 81, 85, 88, 96, 102, 105, 107, 132, 154.
American affairs, 37, 38, 41, 43, 64, 106.
American agents, 41.
"American Archives," 212.
American artists, 175.
American bishops, 76, 77.
American cause, 34, 84.
American Colonies, 14, 34, 49, 57, 75, 76, 84, 99, 104, 105.
American Dictionary, 165.
American episcopate, 51, 98, 99.
American independence, 177.
American liberty, 86, 87.
American States, 137.
Amherst, General, 24.
Andrewes, Bp. Launcelot, 186.
"Antiquities of Canterbury," 80.
"Appeal to the Public," 51, 52.
Apthorp, Rev. East, 199.
Arians, 97.
Articles of Confederation, 119, 123, 126.
Auchmuty, Rev. Samuel, 30, 40.

B.

Bailey, Justice, 171.
Baldwin, Rev. Ashbel, 179.
Bancroft, George, 111.
Barclay, Rev. Dr., 29.
Barnes, Dr., 173.
Barre, Colonel, 32, 59.
Battle of Lexington, 109.
Baxter, Mr., 63.

Beach, Rev. Abraham, 152, 163.
Beach, Rev. John, 9.
Beach, Mrs. Mary, 179.
Beach, William, 9.
Bearcroft, Dr. Philip, 5, 6.
Belden, Esquire, 162.
Belish, Marshall, 26.
Belknap, Dr. Jeremiah, 149, 150.
Bell, Mrs., 40.
Benjamin, George, 113.
Benson, Mr., 66.
Berkeley, Bishop, 4, 91.
Berkeley, Mrs., 63.
Berkeley, Rev. Dr. George, 53, 54, 59, 62, 66, 80, 81, 86; letters of, 92, 93, 96–98, 105–108.
Bernard, Governor, 201.
Billetting Act, 47.
Blatchford, Rev. Mr., 158, 160.
Bowden, Rev. Dr. John, 176.
British Empire, 92, 211.
British Government, 35, 76, 186.
British ministers, 104, 105.
British Parliament, 108, 134.
British Provinces, 154.
Broadstreet, Colonel, 28.
Brougham, Lord, 173.
Burke, Edmund, 59.
Burr, Aaron, 190.
Burton, Rev. Dr., 38, 58, 59, 94.

C.

Cathedrals, 68, 199.
Chalmers, Dr., Thomas, 172.
Chancellor of the University, 151.
Chandler, Rev. Dr., 40, 51.
Chapman, Mr., 40.
Charles I., 71.
Charles II., 177, 183.
Chester, Bishop of, 174.
Chief Justiceship of New York, 45, 47, 98.
Chief Magistrate of Connecticut, 149.